SINGLE DADDY SEDUCTION

A HOT SINGLE DAD ROMANCE #4

ANGEL DEVLIN

TRACY LORRAINE

Editing by Andie M. Long

Cover design and formatting by Dandelion Cover Designs

A NOTE

Single Daddy Seduction is written in British English and contains British spelling and grammar. This may appear incorrect to some readers when compared to US English books.

Angel & Tracy xo

1

SARAH

"She hit me, Daddy. She hit me."

"No, I didn't." I protested looking at Jim's face. "Why on earth would I do that? I've looked after Melinda, Jessica, and Lana for three years, surely you're not going to believe her." But I looked at his face and knew he did. "Look, just give it an hour and I'll sit in my room and then ask her again. She'll change her mind and then she can apologise and..."

"I've called the police."

My jaw dropped. "You've done what?"

"My daughter says you hit her earlier. On the back and on the leg. I asked if you'd hit her before and she said yes."

I looked at Melinda. Nine years old, she'd always been a nightmare to look after. Demanding, argumentative. Lots of, 'You're not my mum'. No, Mummy was too busy running a magazine to be at home and if this is what her version of parenthood was like I couldn't blame her. But I thought we'd been getting somewhere. I mean it had been three years for goodness' sake. But now, for whatever reason, Melinda had told a lie that I wasn't sure we could ever get back from.

My face paled as the thought came, what if the police believed her?

"Please wait in your room until the police arrive. Be packing your bags and then once they've left, I'd like you to leave. I won't of course be paying you for this last month."

The way Jim looked at me was soul destroying. He and Kelly had been so grateful they'd said for my patience with their children and for my not leaving them when other nanny positions became available. Good nannies were hard to find and so we could basically choose our own wages and perks.

As I sighed and made my way up to my room, I walked past Melinda who gave me a satisfied smirk.

I was sure she wouldn't be looking that happy

2

when mummy and daddy found out the truth. God, I hoped they did.

"WOULD YOU LIKE A COFFEE, MADAM?" I look up at the woman dressed in her rail uniform. I'd splashed out even though I was minus my latest wage and upgraded to first class for the journey back to my parents' house in Twickenham from Crewe. Hellishly, my journey from Oxenholme to Crewe was spent sat near a screaming kid and I'd had my fill of children for now.

I accepted a coffee but said no to a muffin. The thoughts of what had happened yesterday afternoon were still at the front of my mind. I just kept ruminating. Seeing the situation again and again and again. The police had been and said there was no evidence, but in the circumstances they understood the parents' concerns and investigations would be ongoing. I wasn't sure what they meant but would look into my own legal action from home. My phone had beeped incessantly since as the local nannies got the goss and tried to find out the truth. None had been my friends. Everyone in the nanny world was a competitor, friendly until they wanted your job and then they'd try to swoop in.

AFTER SPENDING the night in a budget hotel and not getting much sleep, first thing this morning I checked out and got on a train home. My parents didn't know I was coming. The last thing I needed was my mum wittering down the phone last night. I'd needed time to think things over. The situation seemed better explained face to face. Thank goodness I still had my room at their house; a base where I could decide what I did next. Fact is, I had fuck all chance of a nanny job, or maybe any job, while 'investigations continued' and the little savings I had amassed wouldn't last long.

What the fuck was I going to do? All because of a spoilt, lying brat. I was done with kids. Done. Did not want to spend my time with anymore brats anytime soon.

Almost home, I catch a cab from the station down to my parents semi-detached on Lincoln Avenue. As it pulls up outside the driveway and I see the familiar porch, a huge sigh of relief floods through me. I'm home. My parents will know what to do and they'll welcome me in their loving arms.

They never wanted me to go there in the first place; my mum felt it was too far away. I'll spend some time letting them spoil me and then hopefully the recent incident will blow over and I can start afresh.

I ring the doorbell, but no one answers. Shouting comes from inside the house and my brow furrows. Then I hear an ear-piercing shriek.

"Can someone get the goddamn door while I put the dishes away and get a wash on, or am I the only one around here capable of doing anything?" I hear my mum shout. My mum never shouts. What on earth is going on?

Finally, I hear footsteps. "If this is a Jehovah's Witness or some charity collector, I'm going to give them a right earbashing." I hear my younger brother say.

What's Luke doing here?

The door opens and my brother peers at my face.

"Haven't you got a key?" He turns towards the house before he hears my answer, that my mother took it because she lost their spare and has never replaced it.

"It's Sarah." He yells.

There's another scream and my two-year-old

niece Marley comes belting through, not a stitch of clothing on.

"Auntie Say-yah." She flings herself at my legs and the chocolate mousse she had around her mouth transfers straight to my skinny jeans. Fabulous.

"What are you doing here?" Luke asks me.

"Can I actually get through the door, or are you keeping me outside all day?"

He steps back so I can finally walk inside, picking up Marley who wails at being separated from my leg.

I drag my cases inside, rolling my eyes at him picking up his kid instead of my cases. Then again, did I really want coating in more chocolate mousse? It hasn't escaped my notice that my wishes to be child free have immediately been thwarted, but a visit from my brother and niece is nice. I don't get to see them much.

"Where's Liv?" I ask as I walk into the living room, looking around for my brother's partner. They've been together since they met at school at sixteen. Marley came along when they were twenty. Liv calls their relationship passionate. I call it being at loggerheads a lot.

"She's in bed. She's feeling sick."

"Oh poor thing. So you got here and she was taken ill? Does she need a doctor?"

My mum walks in, drying her hands on a dishcloth. Dad bought her a dishwasher, but she refuses to use it, says it doesn't clean properly.

"Sarah! Why didn't you tell me you were visiting?"

"Well, that's the thing. Is Dad here?"

"He's at work, darling. Which is where I thought you'd be."

"Yes, well, I've had to take some time off, so I've come home. I'll be back a while. If it's okay, I'll just go run upstairs with my things."

"You can't." My brother tells me. "I've already told you. Liv's in bed."

"She's in my bed?" I'm aghast.

"No, she's in our bed. That's where we've been staying for the last three weeks since we got evicted."

"Come again?" I state. I can see our mother look from one of us to the other and she steps forward, just as she always did when we were about to take a chunk out of each other as kids.

"Luke and Olivia are staying here with Marley for a while. Marley's in Luke's old room, and Luke and Olivia are in your room."

7

I turn to Luke. "Why did you get evicted? It was for arguing wasn't it?"

He looks at the floor confirming everything.

"I don't know why you stay together with all the rowing you do."

"It's just banter. Nothing serious. It's just Liv likes to throw things and she threw a mug and it hit the kitchen window."

I stand up straight and move into his personal space. "Well, you're all going to have to pack yourself into your old room because I'm back."

"I'm not moving Liv. She's got to be looked after in her condition."

Please God no.

"What condition?"

"She's six weeks pregnant."

I breathe audibly through my nose. "Why has no one told me any of this? That you've been evicted and that Liv's preggers again? That you're staying at our parents' house?"

I look accusingly at my mother.

She just shrugs her shoulders. "We didn't want to worry you while you were so far away, so we just figured we'd catch you up on things when you next came for a visit, and here you are and now you're all caught up."

Is my family for real?

"So I can't stay here then? In my own room. Because my brother has two rooms."

"Of course you can stay. Don't be silly, Sarah. We have a perfectly good sofa. You can sleep in the living room for now. How long were you thinking of staying?"

Well it had been for a while.

"I don't know. How long are you staying?" I ask my brother. "Is there a chance I'll get my room back anytime soon?"

"We're not looking for anywhere until Liv starts feeling better."

I stamp my feet. Twenty-five and stamping my feet like Marley.

Talking of Marley...

"Where's your daughter?" I ask Luke.

He looks around. "Oh shit, and she still has the chocolate mousse."

"Marley?" He shouts running into the hallway.

Me and mum follow him out and find Marley in the downstairs toilet smearing the remainder of her chocolate mousse all over the walls and floor. It looks like shit is coated everywhere but luckily it smells far nicer.

"How has it spread so far?" Luke wails.

"Did she actually eat any of it?" I laugh.

"It's okay for you laughing. You don't have to clean it all up do you?"

"I'll get a cloth." My mum says.

"You'll not clean it up either." I hiss at Luke. "You'll get Mum to do it. You've always been lazy. It wouldn't surprise me if you got evicted on purpose while Liv's out of action so you can get Mum and Dad doing everything for you."

"Get lost. Why aren't you at your hoity-toity job anyway? Slumming it back here, aren't you?"

Something in my expression must give the game away.

A slow smile builds on his face. "Have you lost your job?"

"Sssh."

"Oh wow, the golden girl isn't so golden after all."

My mum comes through with a wet cloth. "Everyone out so I can deal with this."

"Luke should be doing it." I protest.

He picks up Marley. "I have this one to clean up."

"You should clean the toilet walls first."

"It's fine, Sarah." My mum says. "It's just

chocolate mousse. If it was another brown substance, I'd leave Luke to it."

Luke smiles at me victorious until Marley lets out a fart and follows through.

"Oh dear. I'd better leave you to it." I smirk back. "Thought I was the one having a shitty time of it, but it looks like I'm not alone."

2

EMMETT

I blow out a frustrated sigh as the one-year-old in my arms finally falls asleep just as her twin starts stirring.

This has pretty much been my life for the past six months, ever since I put the twins into their own room. If one's peacefully sleeping then the other one is waking, ready to raise the roof with their cries.

I'm exhausted. To look at me, anyone would think I'm approaching my fiftieth birthday not my fortieth. The bags under my eyes have bags and the fine lines I'd been accumulating before Louisa fell pregnant now seem to be getting deeper with every day that passes.

"Just let me stay and help so you can at least

get a few hours sleep tonight," Mum says, poking her head into the twins' nursery with her coat in her hand.

"No, it's fine. You've been here all day."

I love my mum, I really do. I'm not sure what I'd have done without her this year, but I also need my own space, even if it is with two crying babies. Plus, she's in her seventies; the last thing she should be doing is staying up all night with these two.

"Emmett, there's no shame in admitting that you need a little help."

"I'm aware." I don't mean to snap. She knows this too, but it doesn't stop me feeling awful for doing it. "I'm sorry. I just don't want to put any more stress on your shoulders."

"Emmett, I might be old, but I'm not dying. I'm more than capable of looking after these two for a few hours. I managed just fine with you and your sister."

My stomach twists and my heart drops as her eyes glass over at the mention of my older sister. I know that part of the reason she wants to help out so much is partly due to her death. I was only a toddler myself so I don't really remember her illness but all these years on, she's still not dealt with the loss.

Every time she looks at the twins, I know she sees us as kids. She just wants a repeat where she got to see both her kids grow into adults.

"I know, Mum. You should be enjoying the perks of being a grandparent. You should be able to walk away when things get loud because you've already done it once."

"But—"

"No 'buts'. Get out of here. Go and play bingo or something."

"Bingo! Jesus, Emmett, next you'll be telling me I'm only a hop, skip, and a jump away from pushing up daisies." I lift a brow in amusement and she swats my shoulder. Letting out a frustrated huff, she shrugs on her coat and bids me farewell.

She'll only be gone for a few hours. I could put money on her being here before ten in the morning to help.

The sound of her footsteps down the stairs fills the silent space around me before the bang of her shutting the front door finally wakes Elouise from her fitful slumber.

Smoothly walking between the cots, I carefully place Louis down into his bed praying he stays asleep before turning to my daughter and scooping her up in my arms.

Every bad night we have, I always wonder if it's because they know they're missing their mum. They might never have met her but if anything, they'd have known her better than anyone. They lived inside her for seven-and-a-half months; literally a part of her.

"Hush, little lady. It's okay," I soothe, rocking back and forth, hoping it'll be enough to send her off again.

A little over an hour later, I finally get back downstairs. I walk into the kitchen and take in the clear work surfaces and both the dishwasher and washing machine working away. I told Mum not to do it all, but then she never listens so I don't know why I'm so surprised.

I don't have the energy to find myself some proper dinner. Instead I pull the cupboard open and pull out a packet of crisps followed by a tumbler and the bottle of whiskey I save for bad days when I just need a moment to remember that I'm more than just a single dad to baby twins.

I've just poured a generous amount into the glass when my phone vibrates in my pocket.

Ross: I'm outside.

SMILING DOWN AT MY PHONE, I put the bottle back on the side and head for the front door. Ross is my boss, or at least he was before I took paternity leave for the two monsters upstairs. But more than that, he's a good friend, and luckily for me, he seems to have a sixth sense for when I need someone to talk to.

Pulling the door open, I smile and gesture for him to come inside. He doesn't say anything until he's placed the bag he was carrying down on the kitchen counter and I've shut the door. He's been here enough times when the twins are asleep to know not to make any loud noises.

"You look fucking rough, mate."

"Thanks. Drink?"

"Always. I brought curry. Assumed you wouldn't have eaten yet."

"You'd assume correctly. I've only just got them both down."

"Grab some plates then."

I do as he says and watch as he dishes up, the

scent of curry making my mouth water and my stomach growl in anticipation.

He's been known to turn up with some of his wife's leftovers before now, but this whole bringing around a takeaway is new, and it makes me curious.

"To what do I owe the pleasure?" I ask when we're sitting ready to eat.

"I needed some peace and quiet."

"So you came here?" I ask with a laugh. This kind of silence is a rare thing in this house these days.

"I decided noisy babies was better than arguing adults."

"Go on," I mumble around a mouthful of chicken bhuna.

"Sarah randomly appeared this afternoon. She lost her job and turned up expecting her bedroom to be waiting for her."

"But Luke's taken over that room," I helpfully add.

"Right. It's not gone down well. Sarah and Luke are fighting like cat and dog. Marie is about to blow. It's like having two damn teenagers again. I thought when they moved out that we'd be able to enjoy some peace but that's yet to happen."

"So what you're telling me is that this will

never be over," I gesture to the ceiling to where the twins are currently still sleeping soundly.

"Never, mate. Never. Even when they've got kids of their own it seems you can't get rid of them." Ross shakes his head as if he can't believe what his life has become. "You found a nanny yet?"

"I've interviewed about a million." Images of some of the incapable candidates I've been forced to endure over the past few weeks run through my mind. I don't think I'm being picky wanting to find the perfect nanny for the twins and I really didn't expect it to be this much of a challenge. But if they're going to be bringing up my kids and living in my house then the person needs to be perfect. I can't come home after a long day at work to screaming kids and an incompetent nanny; some of which looked like they could well be crying right alongside the kids.

"And?"

"All shit."

"Emmett, you're going to have to do something. You're due to start back at work in two weeks.

"I know." He doesn't need to remind me. The date has been burned into the back of my mind for months. I've been counting down, dreading the day that I'm forced to leave the twins in someone else's care while I earn some money. I've been doing the lottery—something Louisa hated—in the hope I might just win and be able to continue being a stay at home dad, but alas, my numbers are yet to come up.

"You got any more lined up?"

"Nope. And I'm adamant that I'm not allowing my mother to do it."

"She's offered though?"

"Of course. She brings it up at least once a day. But she's too old to be running after toddlers. It's not so bad while they're babies, but as soon as they're walking they'll be running rings around her. I need someone young and energetic."

"I bet she loved it when you explained that to her."

"Not so much. I've no idea what I'm going to do."

"You want Sarah? Christ knows I need her out from under my roof and it's only been a day."

"Uh..." I stutter, unsure how I feel about where this is going. It's fine turning away strangers, but how am I meant to tell my best friend and boss that his daughter isn't the one to look after my kids?

"She got the sack after being accused of hitting some kid apparently. I don't know. It's all a load of bullshit if you ask me. Sarah refuses to even squash a fly let alone hurt a kid."

"She was what?" I ask, shocked. From what he's said about her, she's always seemed so... sensible.

"Accused of smacking a kid. There's no way. She's wanted to be a nanny since she realised what one was. She wouldn't put her career in jeopardy like that. I'd put my life on the fact the little shit is lying. So what do you say?"

"I... uh... I guess I could meet her, maybe?"

"Fantastic. Tomorrow morning. I'll tell her that if she does well, she might be able to get off our sofa sooner than she thinks."

My heart races as my fingers grip the cutlery in my hands a little tighter. This is a bad idea. A terrible idea.

Our peace lasts another thirty minutes. Just enough time to finish our curry and to have a drink. Then both of the twins start up and I'm forced to say goodbye to Ross to deal with them both.

I end up falling asleep in the rocking chair that's placed between their two cots and when I wake a few hours later to Louis crying, it's with a stiff neck and a bad back. Just what I need on top of everything else.

I eventually stumble into my own bed sometime after four in the morning and by some miracle the next time I look at the clock, it's gone nine.

The house is still in silence as I roll over and stretch out my aching muscles. I really want to close my eyes and fall back to sleep but I know it would be pointless. I'd put money on me just drifting off when a little voice will come through the monitor. There are days when I swear they use that thing to watch me not the other way around.

Knowing I'll fall back asleep if I stay between the warm sheets any longer, I drag my tired arse out of bed and into the en suite to start my day.

I have a quick shower and brush my teeth before pulling on a pair of grey joggers and head towards where I can hear soft little voices chatting baby talk to each other.

"Good morning, monsters," I sing, pushing the door open and taking in their happy smiling faces. My heart threatens to burst right out of me when they turn their toothy grins at me.

Every time I look at them, I see her. My wife. Their beautiful mother who never even got a chance to see them. A lump clogs my throat. A year might have passed but the grief never seems to get any easier.

I tickle their podgy bellies as I change their nappies and put them into some clean clothes before scooping them both up into my arms and heading downstairs for breakfast.

I secure them both into their highchairs and set about making their porridge.

The first bowl is in the microwave when the doorbell rings out.

"Come in," I call, assuming it's Mum. She's got a key so can happily let herself in, but she insists on ringing the bell to make sure I'm okay for visitors. I'm not sure what she thinks she's going to catch me up to. The chance to do anything aside from wipe bums and clean up puke would be a fine thing.

I frown when the front door doesn't open like I'm expecting.

"Who can that be? Be good for a few seconds, yeah?" I ask the twins, not that they have a clue what I'm talking about.

There's a small blurred shadow outside the front. Reaching out, I pull the handle and open the door.

"Good morning. Dad said... oh, is this a bad time?"

Her eyes drop from mine in favour of my naked chest and her cheeks heat with embarrassment.

"It's fine. Come on in, Sarah," I say, correctly guessing who she is from a vague recollection of family photos Ross has shown me. I stand aside. "I'll be right back. The twins are through there waiting for their breakfast."

I run upstairs to find a t-shirt. What a great first impression I must be making.

3

SARAH

I have absolutely nowhere to put my things because my brother and his family's stuff is everywhere. I can't get to any of my old stuff in my bedroom because Liv, my brother's girlfriend, is holed up in there, and I've had to put my two cases behind the sofa for now because Marley is trying to open them every five minutes.

And I know I look after kids for a job but when my brother said, 'Fab, while you're here I'm off out for an hour to get a few things we need', I blew up at him, because I'd come to my mum and dad's house for what I'd hoped would be a little time to get my head together.

"Well, if you don't want to spend time with your niece, I'll take her with me." He guilted me, so of course the next thing I know, I'm spending the next three hours, not one, running around after a tearaway.

When Luke returns, he has no bags but does smell of beer.

"What did you do when you were out? Just go to the pub?" I scream at him.

"What's it got to do with you what I do? I'm an adult."

"You're both acting like children." Mum says coming into the living room. "Now stop arguing and help me set the table for tea."

"Go on." I tell him.

"Just need to change Marley. I'll be back to help in a minute." Luke says. I know full well he'll not be back until he hears the shout that dinner is on the table, the conniving pig.

God, I need to get out of here. I thought I'd be coming back to some peace and quiet, and sympathy for my plight and it's entirely stressful. What with this and worrying about the investigation. Really, I could do with calling my friend Reese, but she just had a baby herself. Anyway, I'm seeing her tomorrow night at her engagement party at InHale, a cool restaurant in London. She's expecting that I got some extra time off from work. I'm not going to ruin her evening tomorrow, but I'll ask if we can get together sometime this next week so I can get caught up with her and have some cuddles with Breanna.

My dad comes home. He owns a small company setting up computer systems. His eyes light up when he sees me and then dull again when he finds out a) I've lost my job and b) I've moved back home.

He's been in the house approximately one hour when he 'suddenly remembers' he'd arranged to take a takeaway around to a colleague's house. With a kiss to my cheek and a "catch up later" he's gone.

I sit at the table in a grumpy mood, feeling like a sulky teenager. "I can't believe Dad went out when I've just come home."

"Yeah, well, Emmett is due back at work in a couple of weeks and Dad's trying to make sure he's completely ready."

I pull a face and then remember who Emmett is.

"Oh God. Is he the one whose wife died giving birth to twins?"

"Yeah. Can you believe it's a year ago now? Emmett's due back off his paternity leave. He and your dad are close. Your dad's worried about how he's going to be leaving the twins with someone else."

"Is Emmett old like Dad then?" I'd never met the guy.

My mum rolls her eyes. "Well, that's charming. Don't let your dad hear you say that. Emmett's a little younger than me and your dad. He's thirty-nine."

"Still old though to have newborns. I mean you and dad are what? Forty-three?" Mum nods. "And you have a twenty-five and twenty-two year old. The guy must be exhausted."

"I'm just going to order a barrel full of anti-wrinkle cream now and look for a place in a care home." Mum fake cries. "We might seem old to you, but we aren't actually old, you know?"

"Yeah, they still shag, I've heard them." Luke announces.

I think I'm going to puke and my mum's face glows with her blush.

I seriously cannot stay here after tonight.

LIV MANAGES to get up around seven pm and of course then isn't tired. Everyone is sitting in the living room, also known as my bedroom at eleven pm. I'd really quite like to have a sleep, bearing in mind I hardly slept a wink last night worrying. But no one is showing any signs of moving their arses from the room. I hear the front door bang shut and Marley, who to me should have been in bed ages ago, shouts, "Grandad."

My dad comes through the door looking a lot happier than when he went out. His eyes are a little glazed.

"You had a good time?" Mum asks him.

"Yup." Dad hiccups.

"Dear God." Mum says. "Sit down while I make you a coffee."

Dad plonks himself onto the seat Mum just vacated.

"Might have got you a job, Sarah."

"What?" My eyes widen.

"Emmett needs childcare for his twins. They're one. He's back at w- work." He hiccups again. "In two weeks."

"Well he won't want me, will he? I've just been accused of smacking a child. No one in their right mind is going to employ me. Especially not an overprotective dad of twin babies."

"He's heard me talk about you for years. He

trusts you haven't done it."

"Then he's stupid."

"Why? Did you do it?"

"No." I shout.

"Well then."

Dad accepts the coffee Mum puts in his hand. "Thanks, love. Emmett's interviewing Sarah in the morning to look after the twins."

"Oh that will be perfect." Mum smiles.

"In the morning?" I shriek.

"Oh yeah, did I forget that? Half-past nine."

He drinks his coffee, passes the mug to my mum and within ten minutes he's snoring on the sofa. It's good that someone can sleep on what's supposedly *my* bed.

By the time everyone actually vacates the room it's gone two am. Finally, I can sleep. The sofa is not the slightest bit comfortable but eventually I manage to drop off.

"AUUUUNNNTTIIEEEE SAYWAHHHH."

A body throws itself at me, making me startle.

"W- what. Oh, hey, Marley."

"Wakey wakey."

"What time is it?" I ask myself because of

course Marley has no clue. I scramble around for my phone. Half past five.

HALF. PAST. FIVE.

I've had just over three hours sleep.

The dulcet tones of Liv throwing up come from down the hallway. Finally, she staggers into the living room finding Marley tucked in next to me on the sofa having handed me a book to read to her.

"Oh fab, you're up. I'm going to go back to bed because I feel like crap. Luke will be up at eight. His alarm's set." With that she walks out of the room, leaving me with a very cuddly, but very awake Marley.

I have to get this job today.

Have to.

Luke finally gets up at half-past eight and I race to get myself ready and off to Emmett's house which is in Fulham. I'm insured to drive my dad's car when I'm at home so I'm outside his house with five minutes to spare. Five minutes for me to straighten my hair and apply some lip gloss. I managed to actually grab a shower due to the fact my parents were having a lie-in with it being a Saturday morning, which has helped me feel a little more awake. That and two coffees.

Finally, I get the nerve up to leave the car and walk up to Emmett's front door. I ring the bell and bite my lip nervously.

The door swings open and I'm faced with a tall man dressed only in grey joggers, although to be honest it takes me a second or two to notice that because I'm a little distracted by the toned abdomen and what seems like acres of smooth, creamy flesh. God, he has a trail of hair leading down into those... that's when I notice the grey joggers. Holy hell. Is this Emmett? It can't be. He's almost the same age as my dad and my dad's got a rounded tummy and a double chin.

I raise my head up to actually look at his face for the first time. I feel my cheeks burn. God, I hope he didn't notice me standing with my mouth open. I see dark hair, and chiselled cheekbones. He might be older but fuck he's hot.

He seems flustered and his head turns back into his house.

"Good morning. Dad said... oh, is this a bad time?"

"It's fine. Come on in, Sarah. I'll be right back. The twins are through there waiting for their breakfast."

With that he's gone, running upstairs.

Hesitantly, I take a step through the front door and close it quietly behind me. It's my intention to stay in the hall until he comes back downstairs but I hear a wail and so I follow the sound through to the kitchen where I find the cutest kids I've ever seen sitting in highchairs. The one who was wailing stops when she sees me, her eyes opening wide. "Hello there." I say, noticing that there's a soft teddy on the floor. I pick it up and hand it to her. "Did you drop your toy?"

I receive a toothy grin.

I look from one of them to the other. Their colourings are similar and they are the sweetest and cutest things I ever saw. My heart breaks that they don't have a mum. Not only that but their mother never got to see the bundles of joy she created. I really hope there is a heaven and she's watching over them.

The smell of porridge is coming from the microwave and I see a lip about to wobble, so I make myself useful, sorting out the porridge and I begin to feed the babies.

Emmett comes crashing back into the room.

"Everything okay?"

"Yep, I've managed to not hit any of them yet."

It just shoots out of my mouth. *Oh for God's sake, Sarah. You might as well leave now.*

Emmett goes over to the kettle, lifts it and takes it over to the tap where he fills it with water before switching it on. The kitchen is bright with white gloss units, taupe coloured walls and an island that the twins are next to.

"Tea or coffee?"

"Tea please. Medium strength, milk no sugar."

"Your dad told me about what happened with your previous employers."

"So why did you invite me here?"

"Because I don't believe them. There was no evidence, right?"

"Right."

"And I know all about you from your dad. So I decided I'd get to know you for myself."

"Huh, I think you're stupid if you don't mind me saying so." As far as interviews go, I'd like to smack myself in the face for my current skills or tape up my own mouth to prevent further outbursts.

His eyes alight with amusement. "Oh, how so?"

God, his voice is all husky. He's really attractive. How can this be? He's old.

"Because I could have hit that kid."

"Did you?"

"No!"

"There you go then. So this is Elouise, whose toy you just rescued. The bear is called Ella and she needs it with her at all times. Then this cheeky rascal blowing bubbles is Louis."

"They're gorgeous."

"Well, I'm biased, but I like to think so."

He finishes making the drinks and hands mine to me.

"So, as your dad no doubt told you, I'm back at work in a couple of weeks, although my first week will be just a few hours a day while I get used to being away from the kids and get back into the swing of things. That gives me time to get a nanny and get them used to the routine I have going."

"So what hours will you be looking at eventually? Like eight am to five thirty pm to fit around your work?"

He shakes his head. "Did your father not tell you? I need a full-time, live-in nanny. Someone who can make sure there's a meal cooked and waiting for me when I get home. Twins and work are going to knock me on my arse, especially at first. I need someone I can rely on; not just a nanny, but someone who can maybe do a spot of ironing and things too." He looks at my face.

"Your dad didn't tell you this, did he?"

I shook my head. "My dad wasn't in much of a state to tell me anything."

Emmett laughs and his bright blue eyes twinkle. "Oh dear. I hope I've not brought you over here for no reason then. It's not simply nannying, although that's the main part of it. You see, although I've learned to be handy around the house, it was always my wife who kept the place clean and tidy. There's no way I'm going to be able to juggle the twins in an evening and housework while being tired from work."

"No, I get it, and I can do all those things. But are you sure you want to consider me for the position?"

"Look. This week, come and spend time with me and the twins. I won't leave you alone with them okay? We'll forget I totally did that this morning while getting a t-shirt. Then we'll discuss things further and by then hopefully your name will have been cleared anyway.

"Yeah, hopefully." I reply. I daren't think of the alternative.

4

EMMETT

Knowing the reason Sarah is currently unemployed should have me sending her away as fast as she arrived in my life, but something stops me. Unlike all the other nannies I've interviewed over the past few weeks she's the only one who seems to belong in this house. I know that sounds crazy, but from the moment I pulled the front door open, I relaxed for the first time in about a year-and-a-half, and when she walked inside, I didn't feel like there was a stranger in the house. I guess knowing she's Ross' daughter has settled something inside of me.

Those feelings only multiplied when I walked back into the kitchen, now fully dressed, to find her expertly feeding both of my little terrors with the porridge I was partway through making.

I've no idea how she does it, but there's no screaming, crying, or point-blank refusal to eat it. I also note as I take a step closer, that the only place there seems to be porridge is in the bowl, on the spoon or in the twins' tummies. How does she do that? Most mornings we all end up basically wearing the damn stuff.

Knowing that I can't stand all day watching her, I put myself to use making us both a drink and leaving her to it.

"So, are you up for me showing you around the house?" I ask once breakfast has been totally polished off and we've moved the twins into the living room to play.

She eagerly nods and gets up from where she was playing with Elouise and her teddy.

"Lead the way."

The sight of her sitting crossed legged on the floor with them did something to me. The only other woman I've seen play with them properly has been my mum. But this... right now, it's different. It's what they need, and I'd be lying if I said I didn't already think Sarah is exactly what I need too. She didn't even blink when I explained what this job would entail earlier where most others turned their noses up at the extra duties I said I needed them to pick up. I've no idea if that's because she's desperate, because from what Ross said about his chaotic house it could well be that she just needs somewhere else to sleep, but I'd like to think it's more than that.

"This is the twins' room," I say, gesturing her to enter.

"How do they sleep?"

"Sleep? Sorry, you're going to need to explain that term to me."

She chuckles at my joke but when she turns back to look at me and my tired eyes, I don't miss the sympathy pouring from her.

"I've got a few tricks up my sleeve we can try. That's if you haven't already," she adds quickly, obviously not wanting to step on my toes, which I like.

"Be my guest. I'd do just about anything for a full night's sleep right now."

"I'm sure I can make that happen for you, Mr Wilson."

"Oh God, no. That makes me sound like an old man. Emmett, please."

She nods, turning back to the room, giving me a

chance to take her in once again. Her petite frame is simply wrapped in a white t-shirt and a pair of skinny jeans, a pair of Converse on her feet. I run my eyes over the soft curve of her waist and I try to remember what it felt like to touch a woman. It feels like it's been a lifetime since I had the chance.

My fingers twitch with my need to find out as my eyes rest on the swell of her arse.

Sadly, I'm not paying enough attention and it's not until she clears her throat that I realise she's turned back around and has caught me red handed.

Heat rises to my cheeks as I fight to find something sensible to say.

"And this is where I'd be able to find you." *Shit. Fuck.* "I mean, this would be your room."

She eyes me questionably for a few moments before following my lead and looking into the generous room complete with a king-sized bed and an en suite.

"Wow, this is stunning. Is it the master?"

"Uh..." I lift my hand to rub at the back of my neck. "Yeah. After Louisa, I..." I cough to clear my throat, the lump that has suddenly appeared blocking any more words from escaping.

ANGEL DEVLIN & TRACY LORRAINE

"It's okay, Emmett. I understand how hard it must still be without her." Her tiny hand rests on my forearm in support, her light-blue eyes soft and understanding as she looks up at me.

"I was uh... going to take the twins to the park. Would you like to come?"

She's silent for a few seconds and I fear I might have overstepped the mark but before long a small smile begins to tug at her lips.

"I'd love to. I don't know this side of town very well. It'll be good to get to know it if—" She cuts herself off, clearly not wanting to assume she might have this job, although I've pretty much already made my decision. She already feels like the jigsaw piece this house has been missing.

COMING to the park is a pretty regular thing for me these days. I try to get the twins out of the house every day no matter what the weather but being able to get them out in the sun always makes me feel a little better about life.

Today though, it's even better.

With the winter sun beaming down on us, Sarah and I stand side by side behind the swings pushing the monsters as they squeal and giggle in

40

delight. My heart swells knowing they're having so much fun and that I don't need to be attempting to keep both swings going at once for a change.

"They really are great kids, Emmett. You've done a fantastic job."

"I can't take all the credit, my mum's been there all the way."

"Don't be so modest. I'm sure she's helped but it's you that's done all the work."

Her words repeat in my head while we stand in a comfortable silence.

Once the twins look like they're about to fall asleep in their swings, we place them back in the double buggy and head off on a walk to hopefully send them to sleep.

"Fancy a coffee?" Sarah asks when we approach a cafe.

"I always need coffee." She laughs holding the door open so I can attempt to get inside.

I've got some great friends but sitting opposite Sarah as she sips at her cappuccino and I practically inhale my double espresso, I can't help but breathe a sigh of relief. She's refreshing. I'm not sure if it's her age or the fact she really does just love looking after kids, but she's a breath of fresh air in what's been a pretty mundane few months for me.

"Aside from the obvious, tell me about your previous employer? What were the parents like? What did they expect from you? This is all new to me and I don't want to ask you anything that's inappropriate."

Her kind smile melts my heart a little. It also beats a little faster when I watch her tongue sneak out to wipe away the milky foam that's sitting on her top lip.

"You don't need to worry, Emmett. I'll pretty much do anything. You'll be paying me to make your life easier and that's what I'd try to do as best I could."

My thoughts head straight for the gutter. I might be getting on a bit these days but fuck if I still don't have a working dick.

"Anything?" I ask, raising an eyebrow. I know it's wrong of me, but I can't help myself.

Her cheeks redden and my cock swells. "Well, within reason, Mr Anderson."

Fuck me.

"Good to know. We'd better get these two back before they wake up and scream bloody murder for some food."

After finishing off her coffee, Sarah shrugs into her coat and I try my hardest to focus on getting the buggy out of the corner I'd manoeuvred it into and not on her movements or the way her t-shirt rises to reveal a slither of toned and smooth skin.

SARAH SAYS her goodbyes to me and the twins when we get back home stating that she doesn't want to take up all of our day and I just about refrain from telling her that she's been the best bit of it so far.

Sadness washes over me as I watch her back off the driveway in Ross' car. The process of employing a nanny has been nothing but stressful up until this point. A few people I'd spoken to that had previously been through it told me that I'd know the one when I met them. I thought they were crazy; I was looking for a nanny not a new wife. But it seems they were on the money because it appears I've found the one. The police investigation in regards to her hitting the previous child aside, of course. Although, I think it's pretty obvious from just seeing her with the twins today that she's not got it in her. I was relatively confident in that fact before meeting her today, now I'm even surer.

Louis stirs beside me and I remember that I was in the process of getting them inside for some lunch. Getting my head back in the game, I focus on the task in hand.

We all eat. Well... I eat while Elouise and Louis mostly throw theirs on the floor. *I bet they wouldn't have done that if Sarah was still here*, I muse as I pick up chunks of cheese from the tiled floor.

By the time I put them down for their afternoon nap I'm exhausted, so the sound of the doorbell ringing out makes me groan in frustration.

Now what?

"Hello." Mum's familiar voice calls.

I don't want to be frustrated because she only wants to help, but I could really do with catching twenty minutes sleep right now.

"Hey, Mum," I say, descending the last few stairs. "They've just gone down."

"You look exhausted. Did you get any sleep last night?"

"I can't remember." It was meant to be a joke but the way my deep voice rumbles out the words it sounds anything but.

"Get back up those stairs. I'll listen out for them."

"It's okay. You don't—"

"It wasn't a suggestion, Emmett," she snaps in her motherly way.

"Fine," I concede, turning on my heels and heading back up the way I'd just come down.

I AWAKE with a start and to the sound of a soft female voice singing. My mind immediately goes back to my dream which embarrassingly involved Sarah. She was in the kitchen, still in her pyjamas, singing to the twins as she made their breakfast. I woke up just as she was about to turn towards me so I could find out just how thin the satin fabric of the cami she was wearing was.

I groan and roll onto my back. My morning—or afternoon—wood tenting the sheets. That is until realisation hits that the voice I can hear belongs to my mother. That puts paid to my overactive, sex-deprived imagination.

When I get downstairs, I find Mum cooking, with Elouise and Louis in their bouncers in the middle of the kitchen. God only knows how she's not tripped over them yet.

"You're going out tonight, Emmett. I'm staying to look after these two."

"No, Mum. You don't—"

"Stop. As your mother I'm pulling rank here. You're exhausted; you've barely been out of the house in weeks. You need to let your hair down, have some fun. Call a friend and organise a night out. If you don't want to do it for you, then do it for them." She looks down at my giggling babies. "They need you happy and right now you're anything but. I know this year's been hard, but please, you need to find your life again. You're more than just a dad."

I don't really have a leg to stand on. She's right and she damn well knows it if her smug little smile is anything to go by. It's time I started figuring out who I am again outside of this house and being a dad. I'm due back at work soon and my colleagues are going to expect Emmett, not Daddy.

"I'll go see what Ash is up to tonight," I mutter, walking back out of the kitchen in search of my phone.

"This place is a little flash for you, isn't it?" I ask, looking around at the swanky bar he's brought me to. It's all polished—non sticky—floors, chandeliers, and mirrored bars. It's not his usual haunt that's for sure.

"I'm meeting a bird here later."

"Ah, now it all makes sense."

"Shut the fuck up. You wanted a night out, I'm giving you a night out, Grandad."

"Don't call me that."

Ash is my closest, and oldest friend. I've no idea how that's happened because we're so fucking different it's unreal. He's the ultimate bachelor, jumping from woman to woman and never settling down with any of them. If I didn't know he was also heading for forty, I'd assume he was still twenty-five the way he acts. You'd also never guess that he's a very successful investment banker by day. Everything about him baffles me on almost a daily basis.

"Whatever, mate. Let's get you a drink and find you some pussy." I cringe at his bluntness,

but I can't argue about needing that drink.

5

SARAH

I'm feeling very confused as I drive back to my parents' house. My meeting with Emmett seemed to go really well and he said he would call me on Monday about my going back to spend more time with the twins.

But he kept looking at me for what seemed like a few extra moments than necessary, and at times I felt he was almost... flirtatious.

Don't be ridiculous. He's a widower desperate for help with his kids.

I think I'm reading more into things than is really there. Maybe because, I confess inwardly, I found him desperately attractive.

Is it because I feel sorry for him though? Am I

attracted because I feel he needs saving? Because there's an underlying vulnerability?

I'm a good girl, always have been, and I like to help people. I'm the one who'll give the last of my money to buy a homeless person a sandwich. I'll donate a tenner I haven't got to cleft palate charities. It's who I am. Is that what I'm doing with Emmett, being charitable?

It's not charitable imagining him fucking you in the hallway.

I shake my head to dislodge my completely inappropriate thoughts and get my mind back on driving.

"How'd it go, sweetheart?" My dad asks the minute I walk in the house.

"I think it went well. I'm going back Monday to spend more time with them."

"That's great, and is my car still in one piece?"

I roll my eyes. "Yup."

I note the silence. "How come it's quiet? Don't tell me, Mum got fed up and killed all three of them."

"Your mum went to the park with Liv and Marley. Your brother is still in bed."

"It's half-past two in the afternoon."

My dad shrugs.

I don't hesitate. I run upstairs to my old room.

"Fuck, it stinks in here." I gasp. The smell of fusty body hits my nostrils. I pull the curtains wide and open all my windows.

"Fuck you doing?" Luke pulls the covers over his head.

"I'm getting to my belongings." I find to my absolute horror that my clothes, shoes, and bags are piled up in the corner of the room. They've put their own stuff in my old wardrobe and dumped mine. And what's that? My Michael Kors bag has what I hope is melted chocolate encrusted all over it.

I pick up my shoes and one by one bounce them off my brother's body. "You're a pig. How dare you treat my stuff like this?"

He gets out of bed, stark bollock naked and I dry heave. "I'm going in the shower. You sort your stuff out. It's in our way."

My mouth is wide open as he grabs a robe from the back of the door—my robe—and heads out.

"That's my robe." I scream.

He pauses to run the edge of it up his arse crack and then carries on.

I have to get out of here fast, before I really am in trouble for hitting someone.

I pile my stuff behind the sofa along with all my other belongings and hope it's safe there for now. Over the next couple of days I need to get it all sorted through, washed if needed and packed away. No doubt some of it's ruined. I just daren't look too closely yet.

THAT EVENING it's my friend Reese's engagement party. I treat myself by booking a hotel for the night in central London as it's a train and Tube journey to get there from Twickenham. I move my belongings around and pack a small case with a change of clothes for the evening and the gifts I have—an engagement present for the happy couple and some clothes and a toy for their baby daughter—and I start my journey to the hotel.

I only picked a budget hotel, but it still cost enough in the centre of London. However, the room is large and has a sofa and table in it, the usual kettle to make a hot drink, and most of all a double bed all to myself and peace and quiet. I dump my case down and throw myself across the bed. God, what a difference a couple of days makes. The last time I was in a hotel room I spent the night worrying and sobbing my heart out. Now I feel a tiny bit of hope for my future. Anyway, tonight is about one of my closest friends, not me. I've known Reese since we were kids and I'm so happy she met Brandon and now has her baby though it's been a shock. She was always such a career woman! I can't say I've given being a parent much thought. I've not had any major relationships and I've kind of always worked and thrown myself into being part of other people's families. I really hope I get the job with the twins. That master bedroom was like this hotel room. All that space, just for me.

There's a buffet at the restaurant which I know will be excellent as Jenson Hale's place is the hottest ticket in town at the moment, but I still eat a packet of crisps and a Twix while I have two cups of coffee using my hotel kettle. By the time I'm ready to go to the party I'm buzzing. I decide I'm going to let my hair down and enjoy myself, let the alcohol mellow me and forget my troubles for a while.

Of course I don't bank on the fact that my friend can read me like a book.

"Sarah." She squeals, coming over and

wrapping her arms around my shoulders. "You're here." I hug her back in return. It's been three months since I last managed to see her in real life, just after the birth of Breanna. She's glowing and I'm so happy for her. It makes me tear up a little bit.

"What's wrong?" She says looking me directly in the eye. *Fuck!*

"Nothing. I'm just happy for you. This is your night and I'm ecstatic that you got your man and your baby. Now let's get on with celebrating. I put your engagement gift on the table over there, but I have something for Bree. Where is she?"

"Don't bullshit me. I know you. What's wrong?"

I sigh. "Okay, fine. But please don't make a big deal about it. We'll talk about it properly once tonight is over." I feel the tears threatening again. Bloody eyes. I didn't want to do this at my friend's celebrations. "I lost my job." I confess.

"Oh fuck. I'm so sorry. Why?"

"A misunderstanding."

Reese narrows her eyes at me, but I shake my head. I don't want to do this here, not tonight. Giving in, Reese links my arm with hers and drags me further into the room.

We're halfway to the bar when I freeze.

"What's wrong?" Reese asks me for the third time in as many minutes. I can feel the blood draining from my face. Just what I fucking need right now. Fate is screwing with me big time.

"It's n- nothing."

"Sarah?" a voice from the past asks. My ex, Scott, dressed in the uniform of InHale stops, a plate of canapes in his hands. His brows are drawn together as he looks me up and down.

"Christ, could my life get any worse?" I mutter. "I need a drink. Now."

I drag Reese towards the bar, cutting Scott dead. I have no wish to talk to him.

"Don't," I warn when I open my mouth to ask. "Add it to the list of things to ask me tomorrow."

I turn the conversation to Bree, and Reese opens the gifts I bought her. We go over to the little lady herself and I have cuddles.

"Can I borrow my girl?" Brandon interrupts and I nod and step back as he takes Reese in his arms ready for a dance.

I don't stay much longer. After telling Reese I have a headache, I know she doesn't believe me, but she hugs me and tells me she'll call me tomorrow. I tell her there's no rush, that tomorrow should be spent nursing a hangover and in bed with Brandon. She laughs, reminding me that with a newborn baby there's fat chance of either of those things happening. It makes me think of Emmett. Does he ever get out? Or is his life completely owned by his two babies? If I get the job, I'll make sure he can get out on an evening occasionally. It's at the point I see Scott making his way over to me that I slip out of the exit and make my way out into central London.

It's only nine thirty. I don't want to go back to my hotel room yet. It doesn't have a mini-bar in the room and I'd only lay there feeling sorry for myself. I decide—with the help of the two glasses of wine in my system, and only the crisps and chocolate in my stomach as I've missed the buffet —to head into a nearby bar that looks really swanky and have another glass of wine before I head back.

It's busy but I find a seat at one end of the bar and after ten minutes I manage to get a glass of white. I'm near the male bathrooms so there's a lot of coming and going near me, but I'm still proud of myself. I'm out in central London on my own enjoying a drink. Go me. Maybe this is the start of a new era. A new more confident Sarah? I'm two more glasses of wine down before long and feel fabulous and relaxed.

"Sarah?" I hear.

Huh? Who can possibly know me here? I shrug to myself. It's a popular name.

Then someone taps my shoulder from behind me.

I swing around on my stool to find myself face to face with Emmett.

"It is you." He says. "You look so different all dressed up, but I was just coming back from the bathroom and I recognised your handbag funnily enough and then you scratched your ear. You do it in this particular way..." He trails off. "Sorry, I sound like a stalker. I've not followed you. I'm here with a friend. Of course, I can't prove that because my friend just hooked up and left me. I was just going to the bathroom before making my way home."

"Want a drink?" I ask, the wine mellowing me. "I don't think you're stalking me. I think fate brought you here. Fate is fucking with me. Oops, sorry for swearing. Tonight I saw my ex. Bastard. Anyway, I came here for a drink."

Emmett looks around. "Who are you with?"

"I'm on my own. Been to my friend's

engagement party but had to leave. They were all too happy, you know and then my ex was there and I didn't want to have to deal with him today, so I came out because I have my own hotel room tonight. Just me, no nightmare noisy family and having to sleep on the sofa. So here I am, with wine." I hold up my glass but it's empty.

"Oh."

Emmett laughs. "I'll get you another, but this will probably be your last one okay? Then I'll make sure you are safely delivered to your hotel room."

I pinch his arm. "Are you real?"

"Well that really fucking hurt so let's say yes."

I clasp a hand over my mouth. "You swore!"

"Yeah, I do that a lot, although not around the twins. I'm a normal bloke you know?"

"Oh I know." I say looking him up and down, hopefully without him noticing, only my eyes seem to be a bit stuck on his groin area. Oh dear. Is that his cock or a roll of banknotes? Eyes up, Sarah.

"So why do you wonder if I'm real?" He's laughing now. His face is lovely.

"Because you might be giving me a job, and then you have magically appeared here tonight. So I'm wondering if you are real."

"I'm here tonight because my mother forced me out and this is where my friend chose."

"But what a coincidence you're here and I'm here."

"True. Maybe fate is fucking with us." He says.

Emmett gets us both a drink and I hold up my glass to his. "To fate and fucking... hic... it up." I say.

6

EMMETT

It's true what they say. Having kids makes you a serious lightweight. Before we started trying to conceive, Louisa and I would easily polish off a bottle of wine a night between us, but now, a couple of beers and I'm three sheets to the wind already. It's partly why I didn't believe my own eyes when I thought I saw Sarah sitting here at the end of the bar nursing an empty glass. I thought I was losing my mind. She's not been far from my thoughts since she left earlier. In my drunken state I could quite easily believe that she was a figment of my imagination.

Ash's woman of the night showed up not so long ago with a friend in tow. From the smile he gave me as he greeted them, I'm guessing that was planned for my benefit. Unfortunately for him I have standards, and sadly the friend didn't do it for me. She was pretty, sure, but she wasn't my type. It didn't bother Ash; he took them both home.

The petite brunette that's currently drinking her new glass of wine beside me like it's about to go out of fashion, however, most definitely takes my interest. It's totally inappropriate seeing as I'm intending on offering her a job that involves living under my roof. But I refuse to allow my twins to settle for anything less than the care they deserve. Anyway, she's probably got a boyfriend. *She just told you about her ex,* a little annoying voice pipes up in my head.

"Soooo..." I slur slightly as I try to get my brain to come up with something sensible to say. "Must have been a rocking engagement party if you're drinking alone by ten o'clock."

"I'm sure it was fun enough. I just couldn't hack it. I'm now very glad I left though. I'm enjoying my present company much more."

She's drunk. If her slow speech wasn't evidence enough, her wild, glowing eyes sure tell me all I need to know.

"So if you could be doing anything tonight, what would it be?"

"This is pretty perfect." She tips her glass towards me, successfully managing to slosh wine all over her hands and the bar. "I just need to forget my shitty life where I've got a police investigation hanging over my head and the fact I saw my brother butt naked mere hours ago." Her entire body shudders in disgust and I can't help but laugh.

"I bet that was disturbing."

"You've no idea. He doesn't even have abs like someone else I know." Her eyes drop to my stomach, making my temperature spike a few notches.

Nope, allowing her to look at me like she is now is anything but a good idea.

"I need to use the ladies."

After tipping back the rest of her wine, she wiggles until her high-heeled covered feet hit the floor. She's unsteady and it takes a few seconds too long for her to right herself. Just the right amount of time it takes for me to run my eyes up her curvaceous legs until they hit the high hemline of her little black dress. Surely it's not meant to be that short? It's almost obscene. She drags up some weird need within me to cover her up so other men can't see her exposed skin.

My fingers twitch to reach out to pull the fabric down, but thankfully she beats me to it.

"I'll be right back," she slurs, stumbling towards the toilets.

Sitting back on my stool, I gesture to the bartender. Luck must be on my side because he comes right over.

"This one's on me," he says pouring me a generous measure of whiskey. "I'd need a stiff one if I had to deal with my daughter looking like that."

My chin drops, I know I'm older than Sarah, but I didn't think I looked *that* old.

"Oh no, she's not my—"

"Oh, Christ. I'm sorry. Me and my big mouth. I'll be asking a fat woman when she's due next. Fair play to you, mate. You got yourself a real little treat there." I sense Sarah step up beside me as the entire left side of my body burns with awareness. That heat soon forms in my belly when I see the way the barman runs his eyes over every inch of her.

A low growl rumbles up the back of my throat. I'm just about to say something, fuck knows what, when he's thankfully distracted by his swamped colleague.

"He was hot. You reckon he'd give me his number?" Sarah asks.

"We're leaving."

Turning to look at her, I find her hard eyes narrowed at me. "What crawled up your arse while I was in there?"

"Nothing. You're drunk. I need to get you back."

"Fine. As long as we can still have fun because I'm having a good time."

I'm too busy trying to keep images out of my head that shouldn't be there to notice her reach out and down my whiskey.

"Hey, that was mine."

She shrugs and rolls her eyes. "It was one for the road. Are you taking me home now?"

Ignoring her inappropriate comment and the lustful look that appears to have descended on her face, I pull my phone from my pocket and open up my Uber app.

"Where are you staying?" I ask, refusing to look up at her.

"Give it here." She snatches my phone from me and types in her destination. "Two minutes. Let's go." She singsongs.

Thrusting my phone back at me, she links her

arm through mine and turns us towards the exit. I feel eyes burning into my back and when I look over my shoulder, I find the barman nodding at me with a wicked smile twitching the corner of his lips.

If only I could, I think as I walk beside her, the sweet scent of her perfume filling my nose and making my skin tingle with awareness.

I really need to get laid.

The Uber pulls up just as we step onto the pavement. I lean forward and pull the door open for her.

"You're such a gentleman, Emmett. Are you always that way?" her eyes drop, roaming around my body again.

"Get in."

She follows orders and scoots over to the other side of the car.

"What are you waiting for?"

"N- nothing," I stutter as I wonder how bad an idea being in this enclosed space with her is going to be.

I fight to drag in the air I need once I'm inside the car but it's like it was all sucked out the second I pulled the door shut behind me.

Once Sarah's confirmed where we're heading,

silence falls over the car. The sound of her increased breathing seems to get louder and louder, taunting me, calling to me. Clenching my fists, I fight to stay exactly where I am, staring out the window at the city whizzing by.

"Thank you," she says softly, dragging my eyes over to her.

"What for?"

"Everything. For believing in me when you don't even know me. For turning my evening around."

"It's nothing." I shrug, trying not to make a big deal out of something that felt so natural.

"It means everything to me. You've no idea what the last few days have b- been l- like." Her voice cracks and my heart breaks for her. Being wrongly accused of anything must suck; but being accused of smacking a child and losing not only your job but possibly your career would be devastating.

I hate the tears that fill her eyes. Every muscle in my body aches for me to comfort her, to reach out and try to make it just that little bit better but I know I shouldn't.

"I'm sorry. This isn't a great impression I'm

giving you right now. You'll never want to employ me after seeing me in this state.

"Sarah, that's not—"

"Here you go. I hope you enjoy the rest of your night."

Looking up, I realise we're outside Sarah's hotel.

"Thank you."

Without thinking, I jump from the car and race around to her side to help her out. Thank fuck I do because she only manages to get half her foot on the pavement and very nearly tumbles to the ground.

Reaching out, I wrap an arm around her waist to stop her from falling. A spark shoots up my arm. It's so strong that I almost release her again but the second she turns her wide, panicked eyes on me, I manage to regain some kind of composure. That is until I right her and she stumbles forward against my chest.

I gasp, the feeling of her curves pressed up against my body is a little too much to handle, especially with the amount of alcohol that's currently running around my system.

Her head lifts, her eyes taking in every one of my features before they land on mine. The light blue I admired earlier has given over to a darker hue that threatens to drag me in even deeper.

Her tongue sweeps across her bottom lip and I'm mesmerised by the movement, wondering how sweet it must taste.

I'm so close to leaning down and finding out when another car pulls up out the front of the hotel and the person getting out opens their door on Sarah. I jump back and pull her with me.

"Oh my god, I'm so sorry," the lady vacating the taxi says, looking horrified.

"It's okay," I say, before turning back to Sarah who's crashing and fast. Her eyelids are starting to lower and she's leaning on me more and more for support. I can't deny it doesn't feel fucking fantastic, but I need to do what's right by her. "Come on, let's get you to your room. I think it's time you slept off that wine."

With my arm wrapped tightly around her waist, I walk us over to the lifts and hit the button for the fourth floor when she mumbles it at me.

She slumps back into the corner of the lift and I fear that if I weren't here she'd probably end up spending the night there.

"Come on, sleepyhead." She moans when I pull her from her corner and down the corridor.

"Which one?"

"Ummm..." She stumbles in her heels before dropping to the floor and uncoordinatedly pulls them from her feet in a huff. "I don't know," she sighs in defeat.

"Do you have the key?"

"It's in here." She throws her bag somewhat in my direction and I bend down to pick it up.

I hesitate. I'm not the kind of man to go rummaging through a woman's bag but when I look up and find her falling towards the wall with her eyes shut, I realise I don't have a lot of choice.

Unzipping it, I rummage through until I find a folded bit of card with the keycard inside.

Room 446.

Looking up at the door next to me, I realise we've got a bit of a way to go yet.

Hooking my arm through her back, I step up to her but it seems she's totally out of it.

"Fucking hell, Sarah."

Bending down, I scoop her up into my arms. She almost immediately snuggles into my neck and I can't help the wave of contentment that washes over me. It's been so long since I've been held like this. I almost don't want to put her down.

But sadly, before I know it, I'm standing before

her door. Thankfully the keycard is keyless entry so with a tap to the door, I'm pushing inside.

The room's exactly what I was expecting for a budget chain hotel, but what I wasn't expecting was for it to be so tidy. It makes me smile knowing that she's a bit of a neat freak because that's something I need. The twins and I make enough mess as it is; we don't need another adding to the issue.

Dropping her key and bag onto the table, I continue with her in my arms over to the bed. She doesn't wake at all when I lower her down and take her shoes from her hand.

Standing straight, I take a moment to look at her. She's so beautiful, peaceful, and... young. I've no right to be here right now. And especially no right to be looking at her while she's fast asleep with her dress hitched up high around her thighs or feeling the kinds of things I am right now.

How easy would it be to slip in beside her and pull her into my arms? The thought of falling asleep with her has my heart pounding and my cock swelling. But I know I can't.

Instead, I pull the covers over her and take a giant step back to stop me doing anything inappropriate like dropping an innocent kiss to her slightly wrinkled forehead.

With a heavy sigh, I back up to the door. She doesn't make a sound, not until I push the handle down and the click of the lock rings out in the silent room.

"Emmett?" Her voice is soft and rough with sleep.

I still, waiting to see if she's going to say anything else or if she's talking in her sleep.

"Please."

Fuck. My cock swells making my trousers uncomfortable but without another look, I hurry out of her room.

7

SARAH

I wake up, hurtle out of bed, and throw up. I'm hot, sweating like crazy, while my face goes clammy. All this is happening before I can even think straight.

Wiping my mouth with some toilet paper, I lean over the toilet bowl and closing my eyes, try to think.

I'm in the hotel I paid for.

I went to the engagement do.

I saw Scott. That thought makes me groan.

Then I went to the bar, where I met... Emmett.

Cold fear washes through me. What the fuck did I do or say? I don't even remember. I don't even know how I got back to my room.

Looking down at myself, I'm reassured that I'm

still wearing the clothes I had on at the party and the bar. My knickers and bra are exactly where I put them. There's no discomfort from a heavy sex session.

Once my body has finished throwing up, I slowly get to my feet, throw water on my face and brush my teeth. Again, trying hard not to move my head too briskly, I fill the kettle and make myself a strong, black coffee. It's then I notice my shoes at the side of the bed and a memory of taking them off comes to me.

As I lie on the bed slowly sipping my hot beverage, and occasionally cursing about the hammer-attack like headache at my temple, more memories float into my mind. Drinking Emmett's whisky. That must be the drink that took me over the edge. Being in the lift with him, staring at his body. I don't think I said anything inappropriate but what if I did?

The chances are that he now thinks that even if I didn't hit my charge, that I'm a pisshead not capable of taking care of children anyway.

I call reception.

"Good morning, Miss Fletcher. How can I be of service?"

"Is there any way I could extend my stay to a

further evening and check out on Monday instead?" I will have no savings left at all soon, but I cannot survive a hangover at my parents' house, and even more, I don't think I feel well enough to even leave the room.

"Of course. I've changed your booking and checkout will now be noon on Monday. Will there be anything else?"

"No thank you. That's fantastic." I state, and then after drinking my coffee, I pad over to the hotel room door where I hang a 'do not disturb' sign on the outside.

On my way back to my bed I pass the table in my room and find a note scribbled in an unfamiliar hand.

Hope you don't have too much of a hangover!
I hope I don't either!
Let me know you're okay.
Emmett.

UNDERNEATH IS HIS MOBILE NUMBER. I had it in my phone now anyway. Do I call him? Losing my nerve, I text instead.

Sarah: **I'm alive. Barely. You?**

Emmett: **I have twin babies. I am regretting every drop that passed my lips because they woke at 7am, and that's a lie-in for me!**

Sarah: **Well, I just thought I'd let you know I'm okay. Obviously, I'm guessing I embarrassed myself well and truly by being drunk, so I thank you for giving me the opportunity to chat to you about the job and good luck with your hunt.**

Emmett: **What are you talking about?**

Sarah: **A lush who might have hit a kid. Application of the year.**

THERE'S a pause and I wonder if that's the last I'll hear from him, but no, my phone dings again.

Emmett: **We've already discussed 'smackgate'. We'll await the results of the investigation. Last night you were not out at an interview, you were a young woman out enjoying her evening. That's allowed. I was not an employer. I was an old man out having a drink. Apparently that's allowed too, my mum insisted! So, we were both drunk. You just got more drunk because you pinched my scotch!**

Sarah: Erm, yes, sorry about that... My head this morning is even sorrier.

Emmett: Apart from having to take you back to your hotel room, the rest of the night was good fun. I'm aching a bit this morning from having to keep you in a straight line. I'm not used to being with female company that's older than 1 or younger than 76!

Sarah: I just died of embarrassment. I am SO SORRY.

Emmett: Look, in all seriousness, just promise me you won't drink that much again. Not because I'm a potential employer, but for your own safety.

Sarah: I won't, I promise. A) I don't usually. B) I drank more than usual to stay talking to you because I was having fun (I do remember that before it goes blurry), and C) My head is banging.

Emmett: As is mine. Now I will see you tomorrow exactly as we scheduled. I don't even have a liquor cabinet so you're safe here!

Sarah: Okay then. Thank you.

Emmett: I'm hoping to be thanking you by you getting these rogues in order. Louis just filled his nappy so I've got to go. Safe journey home.

Sarah: **I'm staying another night. I daren't move. I just want to sleep and there's no chance of that happening at my parents' house.**

Emmett: **I'm so jealous. Speak soon.**

I PLACE my mobile phone down and think once again about how nice Emmett is. I feel so sorry for him that his wife died. I wonder what she looked like? Slipping down under the duvet as I feel my eyes closing, I drift off, having dreams of Emmett standing at the front of an aisle as his bride walks towards him, but unnervingly she has my face.

I WAKE AGAIN and rub at my eyes as I drag myself up the bed and lean back against the headboard. The alarm clock says it's now 16:04.

Shit! Dragging myself out of bed, I hit the shower, finally taking the party dress off. When I feel better from spending an extended length of time under the soothing warm water, I dress in the fluffy hotel robe and lay on my bed, putting on the TV and looking at my phone. I have a missed message from my mum and one from Reese. I text my mum that I had a good time but that I'm staying an extra night and then after ordering a burger and fries through room service as I'm now ravenous, I phone Reese.

"Hi. Is it a good time to talk?"

"It's a great time. Brandon just took Bree for a walk in her pram and so I have my feet up on the sofa and a sneaky glass of vino in my hand."

"Oh God, don't mention alcohol."

"How come? You left so early you can't possibly have been drunk."

"I went to a bar and had far too many drinks and completely embarrassed myself."

"Oh you have so much to tell me. Right, I'm all ears. Start with how you lost your job."

I tell her about the accusation against me and then how my dad had put in a word for me with Emmett.

"Oh babe, I'm sure it'll all blow over, but if it

doesn't, I know a damn good lawyer." Reese had worked in family law before having Bree.

"Who is on maternity leave."

"If you need me, I'm there for you, Sarah. You're my best friend."

"Thank you. I appreciate it and I love you. You're the best."

"I am. Anyway, what's this Emmett like? Is he fit?"

"He's coming up for forty and one of my dad's friends."

"So? He'll know what he's doing. Is he a silver fox? Or, are you going to disappoint me now and tell me he has six chins and a beer belly?"

I sigh. "No, he's a fox, more dark than silver though. Obviously looking after twins keeps you fit. He looks years younger than my dad, although I guess no one in their right mind looks at their dad through 'is he fit eyes', do they?"

"So... you might be getting a job with a sexy, fit fox?"

"As a nanny-come-housekeeper to look after his twins so he can work and have a bit of a life."

"You could help bring him back to life."

"I think I'll just enjoy having some

employment. That's if the fiasco of 'smackgate' disappears. I pinch Emmett's terminology.

"'Smackgate'. I like it. Oh I'm sure that will get sorted soon. They can't prove what never happened."

"Hope so. Because I need that job. It comes with a room like a hotel suite. I'll be able to escape my parents' house."

"Right, my next question for you. Who is Scott Sullivan?"

I utter a deep sigh down the line.

"It's him, isn't it? The one we aren't allowed to ever talk about."

"I can't talk about him."

"But the chances are I'll keep seeing him. Brandon's friend Aiden's girlfriend's brother owns the restaurant."

"I'm too hungover to follow that, but fine. I'll finally tell you about him as long as then he goes back to being the one we aren't allowed ever to talk about."

"I'm listening."

"This isn't some latest episode of a soap opera you know? It's my life."

"Your life's more exciting than Eastenders lately."

"So, Scott. Before I explain fully. In a nutshell, he took my virginity and then never contacted me again."

"Bastard."

"His auntie and uncle lived next door to our house. At one point Scott stayed with them for a while. Told me his mum was ill. He was seventeen. I was fifteen. At first he just said hello to me a few times over the fence. I got a crush of course because he's devilishly good looking. My mum being an idiot invited him to my sweet sixteenth."

"I remember you talking about the lad next door, and then of course I had flu when it was your sixteenth and bloody missed it all."

"Yeah, well, my party was boring. Well that's unfair but it was family and friends but no best friend and I don't know... I just expected something amazing to happen on that date. Scott stayed long enough to give me a present and then disappeared. Everyone went home and I just told my mum I'd walk back and make my own way home. As I passed through the park, he shouted me. He was leaning next to a tree drinking from a bottle of vodka." My mind went back to that night.

"He offered me a drink and patted the ground next to him. I sat there and drank. He seemed so interested in me. He asked me if I'd got everything I wanted for my birthday and I said no. I wanted a boyfriend and I wanted to lose my virginity."

"You did not say that."

"I did. I blame the vodka. But he was so hot and I just thought if we had sex it not only got rid of my virginity but he'd realise how grown up I was." I groaned. "I was such an idiot."

"So what happened?"

"We made out behind the trees, and then he walked me home. He made me promises about us seeing each other. The next night I snuck into his room and we did it. The day after he was gone."

"Gone as in left?"

"Yeah. I was told by his auntie that his mum was better and so he'd left. I tried to call him and he sent me a text saying it had been fun but he was home now and he hoped I had a nice life. Then he blocked me."

"You're shitting me?"

"Nope. And so when you were better I told you that I lost my virginity but I didn't want to discuss it and the boy would always be the one we never talked about."

"And now he works at InHale. I asked Kaylie about him. She says he's completely in love with himself. Is a total manwhore, but a good worker. And she said you can add another person to the 'hates Scott' list because there's a bartender there called Suki who can't stand him."

"I know we were young but it's a special time for a girl, their first time, and he was just gone. He spoiled it."

"You're such a romantic though. Most people's first time ends up being shit."

"Maybe, but it doesn't sound like he's changed so we still don't like him, okay?"

"Okay."

We chat for a while longer and then there's a knock on the door.

"That'll be my burger and fries turning up, so I'll have to dash." I tell her. We say goodbye and then I let the guy bring in my food, tuck in heartily, and then lie on my double bed watching TV for the rest of the evening.

It's heaven.

And I can't help but think my room at Emmett's would be like this.

I really want that job.

8

EMMETT

"I know I said to go out and enjoy yourself, but Christ, Emmett, you're not twenty-one anymore," Mum chastises when she finds me laid out on the sofa with my phone in my hand.

Don't I know it. If I were young and less sensible I might have gone after what I really wanted last night. My phone buzzes as another message from Sarah comes through and I can't help the smile that spreads across my face despite how much she's suffering for her blow out this morning. She thinks I'll see her differently because of it, but I, of all people, know how important it is to let off steam every now and then, and I know that's all it was. I've heard enough stories from Ross about how his daughter is the sensible one while his son is out doing all sorts all hours of the night. Sarah's life's just been turned upside down; no one would be able to blame her for going a little wild last night.

"You're smiling at that thing like it's just told you that you've won the lottery. Have you met someone?"

"Huh?" I ask, not hearing a word of what she just said. I was too busy rereading Sarah's messages.

"I asked if you'd met someone."

"Oh, no. It's... uh... just Ash."

"Don't tell me, his hangover is worse than yours. Nothing but trouble that boy."

Rolling my eyes, I drop my phone and look up at her.

"He's nearly forty just like me. He's not a boy and he's not trouble. Just because he's decided to live his life as a bachelor and not settle down doesn't mean he's trouble." The words roll off my tongue like I've said them a million times before, which in fact I have. Mum didn't like Ash from the first time he came to our house for dinner when we were thirteen. You'd think she'd have got used to him by now.

The day passes as every day does when there

are babies involved. Feeding, nappy changes, snotty noses wiped, and soft lullabies are sung in the hope of a few hours' sleep tonight. Mum tried to tell me they went down easily without me last night but if the bags under her eyes told me anything it was that she was lying. She's desperate to allow me to let her look after them when I go back to work and she's trying to prove she's capable. I feel awful every time her face drops when I repeat my need for a nanny, but I refuse to break. I want her to be a grandma and to enjoy her time with the twins, not be forced to do it. I'd hate for her to ever begrudge spending time with them because she should be out at bingo or whatever old ladies do these days.

"Sarah's going to be spending quite a bit of time here this week, so you don't need to worry about being here so much."

"Oh, I see." Her voice breaks and my heart twists. *This is the right thing to do,* I tell myself and it's not just because you're already excited to see Sarah again.

THE TWINS HAVE A WEIRDLY good night. I'd like to think that with them sleeping I'd be able to as well but in my confusion I find myself awake and staring at the baby monitor or getting out of bed to make sure they're still there and breathing. This means by the time they both wake the next morning, I've not had much more sleep than on a bad night. Having said that though, I do jump out of bed with a little more spring in my step than usual. I tell myself that it's because it's the start of a new week but really I know it has everything to do with our visitor that'll be here in a few hours.

"Good morning, monsters. How are you both after your long night's sleep?"

Excited baby chatter greets my ears and I smile as I set about to get them ready for the day.

Thankfully, by the time the doorbell rings, both Elouise and Louis are playing in the living room and I've managed to clean up both the kitchen and run the vacuum cleaner around. I'm feeling very domesticated. That doesn't mean it's something I enjoy, mind you. Although I'm going to miss the twins like crazy when I go back to work, at least I'm going to be able to hand over a few jobs that I hate. Vacuuming and dusting being two of them.

I've run some wax through my hair, trimmed the scruff on my jaw and even put on my best t-shirt, AKA the one with the least puke staining the shoulder, and I'm almost ready to face her. If only I could convince the butterflies fluttering around in my belly that I was a grown arse man who doesn't need to be nervous about a young woman entering his house.

As I walk towards the front door my palms are beginning to sweat. Shaking my head, I laugh to myself.

"Good morning," she sings in greeting. Her eyes are much more alert than the last time I saw her, but her cheeks are equally as rosy, whether that's from the morning winter chill or her embarrassment, I'm unsure.

"Come on in, we're all ready for you."

"You really haven't changed your mind?" Her voice is light as she asks but it still annoys me. This false accusation has messed with her confidence. Not that I have a clue as to how confident she was before, but I sense she was better than putting herself and her skills down at every possible opportunity.

"Sarah," I say, turning to her. She's not paying attention to the fact I've stopped and she crashes straight into my front.

Dropping my hands to her waist, I steady her

and put a little space between us. Her being close brings back too many cravings that she dragged up on Saturday night. Cravings that I need to forget about while she's here looking after my babies.

"Stop questioning this. From what I've heard and seen, you are an incredible nanny. You're kind, caring, and more than capable of entertaining two little terrors. I understand it's awkward with what's happened, but I really think we could have a good thing here... with you being the twins' nanny, I mean," I add when her eyes widen in shock. "Stop worrying. I think you're incredible—you're going to be incredible," I correct, now starting to panic at my lack of ability to filter what's spewing out of my mouth. "Would you like a coffee?"

"Yeah, please."

"The twins are in the living room in their playpen, unless you'd rather learn where I keep the coffee."

"You look like you could do with a sit down. Another bad night?"

I explain our night while she stands in the doorway watching my every move. She makes no attempt to go and see the twins until I gesture for her to do so and I can only imagine that's because of me saying that I wouldn't leave her alone with them when we first met. I'm relieved as well as frustrated that she feels the need to do that.

"Hello, my little angels. Have you been giving your daddy a hard time?" Sarah coos as she kneels down between them. "Are you having fun with your animals?"

She totally ignores me watching her as she sets about teaching the twins each animal noise and has them trotting around where they're sitting making them both giggle. It's so wonderful to watch and it has a ball of emotion crawling up my throat to the point my eyes get a little damp.

I've no idea how much time passes as I sit there with my cooling coffee in my hands watching the three of them play. But the second she turns and looks up at me it's like time freezes. Her light blue eyes hold and then search mine, her lips parting ready to say something.

I desperately want to look away, to hide the emotion that's so clear on my face but I'm powerless to do so.

"Is this..." she gestures to what she's doing. "Okay?"

"O—" I have to clear my throat before I can get any words to form. "Of course. They love you already."

"I'm not sure about that. They're wonderful. You've done an incredible job."

I nod, unable to voice how much those words mean to me.

When it finally sunk in that my wife hadn't made it through their birth, I had no idea how I was meant to continue alone. I was already terrified at the prospect of having not one but two babies to look after, but suddenly I was expected to take them both home and do it alone.

I thought I'd been scared before. Like when I did a parachute jump a few years ago. I thought that moment of standing on the edge of the plane ready to jump was terrifying, but the minute I stood in the doorway of the hospital that led to the outside world with a bag over each shoulder, and a car seat in each hand with a very tiny person sitting in each, I was trembling with fear. I'd barely held a newborn before; now I was expected to do everything.

The following few weeks and months were a learning curve that's for sure. I had to try to grieve the loss of the love of my life without being able to break down and shut the world out like I craved to do. I couldn't do that to my babies, so I pushed through.

Some days are still incredibly hard, but at some point over the past few months things started to get easier. I began to accept the hand I'd been dealt and I was growing in confidence as a father. I figured that if I could do those first few weeks without losing the plot then I could manage whatever else was to come.

When I eventually go to sip my coffee it's stone cold. "Ugh," I complain, dragging Sarah's attention from the twins to me.

"I'll go and make us two fresh ones." I look over to her mug sitting on the side table and realise hers is still full and cold too. "What time do these two usually have lunch? Would you like me to start preparing something?"

"Uh..." I glance at the clock on the wall. "Actually, they usually eat about an hour ago. It seems you've managed to distract them from their bellies."

"Oh my goodness, I'm so sorry." She looks devastated by the news.

"It's fine. If they were hungry I'm sure they would have found a way to make themselves heard," I say with a laugh, hoping it reassures her.

"I'd just hate to disrupt your routine before I've even started. Assuming I do... start that is.

I'm meant to be learning their routine not ruining it."

"Sarah, calm down. It's fine."

She nods, her eyes flitting from me to the twins who are happily fighting over a rattle.

"Do you want me to come and show you where everything is?"

"No, you stay there and relax. I'm sure I can find my way around your kitchen."

"Shout if you need anything." I'm equally relieved as I am disappointed as I watch her arse sway from the room. A huge part of me wants to melt into the sofa and just take a breath while the other is desperate to be in the kitchen with her, watching as she finds her way around and makes herself at home.

"Here you go, this should keep you all going." She hands me a fresh coffee before passing the twins a beaker of water each.

"Thank you."

"You're more than welcome. Now let me see what I can rustle up."

"Good luck. I've not been shopping for quite a few days."

"I can be pretty resourceful when I need to be. No worries."

9

SARAH

I'm in the kitchen looking through the fridge and cupboards seeing what I can knock up for lunch. I'm enjoying spending time with Emmett and the little ones and I'm certainly in no rush to head back to my parents' house. My case is in the hallway for now. I could have cried when checking out of the hotel. I was in no rush to leave my large peaceful room behind. But back to the sofa I go.

There are plenty of eggs, so I make scrambled eggs for Louis and Eloise and then I slice a pepper and some mushrooms from a half-used packet and make a large omelette for myself and Emmett to share. There's some orange juice so I pour a glass of that each for us and when it's all finished I shout Emmett through.

He sniffs the air appreciatively. "Gosh, that smells good."

"It's only a very simple omelette." I say.

"That I didn't have to cook, and also, if you're wanting to impress me as an employer, I won't have to unload and reload the dishwasher either."

I cock a hip. "Are you taking advantage of me?" I then blush a deep shade of red before adding quickly. "Making me do all these chores."

Emmett moves the twins so I have Elouise at my side and he has Louis at his. "We'll feed one each so we can have our omelettes while they're still warm."

"Are you making this boys versus girls here because I can assure you that us girls will finish with more food in our bellies than on the trays and floor?"

"Well I was just being helpful taking one of the twins, but now you mention it..." He does an aeroplane noise to Louis, "Open wide, Louis, the plane is coming to land."

Elouise just eats hers so by the time I'm up from the table sorting the dishwasher, Emmett is still trying to get Louis to eat because he's insisting that Emmett does the aeroplane at least twice before every mouthful. Neither has he had time to finish his own omelette. I stare at him triumphantly when I'm all cleared up and I walk over to him and hold my hand out for Louis' spoon.

"Get your food finished or you'll still be here while I cook an evening dinner."

"Well if you're offering to cook later as well, I'm not sure that's going to give me any incentive to go any faster."

I catapult a small piece of scrambled egg at Emmett's face. "Behave."

"Says the person throwing food in their potential future employer's face."

"Coffee and a jam tart?"

"I have jam tarts?"

"Yeah there's a full packet in the cupboard."

"Ah, that'll be my mum's doing. She likes to leave me treats when she pops in."

I make us a drink and get the jam tarts box out. I leave the twins in their seats and put a few raisins on their trays for them to attempt to get in their mouths. They're making the cutest little noises.

"Yes, you tell me and Daddy all about it." I chat to them. "So you're obviously very close to your mum?" I say to Emmett as I choose a strawberry tart.

"Yes, sometimes a bit too close though."

Emmett pulls at the neckline of his top. "I don't know what I would have done without her at times, but she's getting older. She's seventy-six now and I've noticed she forgets the odd thing more these days now. She wanted to look after the twins while I return to work and I had to say no. It's awkward but she's very capable of being a grandma, but not a full-time nanny. You understand me, don't you?"

"Absolutely. Plus with a nanny you get the professional boundary of being able to direct them with what you want, whereas your mum's likely to just do what the heck she likes. I mean that's what being a grandma is all about."

"Exactly. I think I've hurt her feelings though."

"She's probably just unsure about the change. It's been you and her for over a year, now someone else might be coming into your home and lives. It's understandable when you think about it. She'll be worried about you and your return to work, worried about the twins being left with a stranger, concerned she'll get to see them less."

"How come I'm so much older than you, but you seem the more sensible, mature one?" He smiles.

I laugh but inside I feel like he's just insinuated I'm some kind of child.

"Talking about age. When are you forty?"

"Stop swearing at me." Emmett covers his ears.

"It's not thaaattt old." I say.

"I'm three years younger than your father. Do you call him an old man?" Emmett raises an eyebrow.

"Erm... no comment."

"Exactly."

"Emmett, you don't look anything like my dad. My dad's got a beer belly. You obviously look after yourself."

"All compliments welcome. Tell me more."

"Absolutely not. You'll get bigheaded."

"My birthday is in February. I have no idea what to do for it or where to go because I'm not sure I even want to celebrate it."

"That place I went to at the weekend was really nice, InHale. It gets booked up crazily though in the restaurant itself so I'm not sure if the function room would be free." I then remember Scott works there. Am I an idiot? Oh well. I'd not actually be there would I? If I got the job I'd be at home looking after the babies.

"Hmm. I don't know. I think I'll get used to working again first and having to deal with grown-ups on a daily basis, then I might brave arranging my fortieth. Anyway, shouldn't I do a parachute jump or spend a day driving a fast car? It's time for my midlife crisis to hit."

We hear a key turn in the lock, and then a female voice shouts out. "Emmett? Are you in?"

Emmett groans. "It's my mum. She knows full well I'm in and she knows you're coming."

I giggle. "She's here to check me out. I love it."

"We're in the kitchen." Emmett shouts. Then he mouths, "sorry," at me.

What Emmett doesn't realise is that this happens to some extent in every job. Extended family members turn up to make sure a serial killer hasn't been left in charge of their nearest and dearest.

An older lady, average height and a little plump, with a grey bob comes walking through the kitchen door. Her brown eyes alight first on the twins and then on me before they fall to Emmett. She's dressed in black trousers and a crimson coloured ribbed jumper over a black polo neck.

"Gosh it's rough out there today." She announces rubbing at her cheeks. "I feel like my face has been sandpapered." She walks over to the twins and kisses each of them. "How're my grandbabies?" she coos.

"Pretty much the same as when you saw them yesterday." Emmett states.

"Yes, darling, that's why I'm here. I seem to have mislaid my glasses case. My DKNY one. Have you seen it? I was shopping and passing and so thought I may as well drop by."

I stand nearer to her now she's finished kissing the babies. "Hello, there. I'm Sarah. I'm just here to meet with the twins with regards to a potential nannying position." I hold out my hand. "It's very nice to meet such an important person in the babies' lives. I hear from Emmett that you have been extremely instrumental in their upbringing and may I say you've done a fine job. They are two beautiful children."

Emmett's mother preens, standing taller. "I'm Diana. It's a pleasure to meet you, Sarah. Yes, I have indeed spent a lot of time with my two gorgeous grandbabies. Now don't take this the wrong way, but I actually don't think Emmett needs someone full-time. I'm used to looking after them."

"You might well be right. It's something for Emmett to consider before he makes his final decision. Now let me get you a drink while you sit with Louis and Elouise. We were just enjoying those lovely jam tarts you bought."

"I do love a sweet treat."

"I bake a lot." I tell her. "I'll have to drop off some of my homemade tarts for you. I know how to get the pastry really short. Anyway, while you enjoy your drink I'll just go run the vacuum around everywhere, and I'll strip the beds, clean the windows down, and then I'll start to prepare the evening meal from scratch because Emmett's told me about how he'd ideally like them raised on all fresh food, so I need to show off my cooking skills. Oh, and I'd better do the grocery shop because you've not got much in." I say to Emmett who is clearly bemused by all my lies as he's not told me to do any of these tasks.

"Oh that might not be necessary, Sarah, not if my mum's going to do everything. Even better, I wouldn't have to pay her."

"Well," Diana says. "It might be that it would be useful to have a little help around the place with the housework and such."

"Well Sarah's a childminder so that will be her out, but yes it's a possibility for me to consider." Emmett joins in. "You could be here from 6am.

That will give me time to shower and leave. Then if you have a meal ready for us when I get home, help me bathe the kids and then you'd be able to go around 8pm? And I'll sort a cleaner to drop by for a few hours and maybe a regular supermarket online shop." He looks at me and shrugs.

"Sorry, Sarah, to mess you around. It looks like I might be covered."

"Well let's not be too hasty." Diana puts her hair behind her ear. "Because the other way of looking at it is, I could simply become the grandmother I've always longed to be, dropping in to pick the kids up and whisk them off to the park or the farm, while allowing Sarah the opportunity to catch up on chores and then I could help Sarah in the kitchen and with feeding one of the babies while she does the other. I could be the same help I've been to you."

"If I got the job, I would absolutely love that, Diana." I hold a hand to my heart. "You'd be able to show me all their routines so that I kept as closely to their usual schedule as possible."

"There we go then." Diana tells Emmett. "Sarah can be the nanny and I can help her, show her the ropes."

"Would you like another coffee, Diana?" I ask.

"I'd love one, Sarah. Thank you, dear." She turns to Emmett. "Well, why haven't you offered this charming girl the job already?"

Emmett rolls his eyes. "Because she's having a trial run, Mum."

"Let me go and see if I can spot your glasses case." I tell her and I leave them to it. Of course I knew there would be no glasses case whatsoever, but it gave Emmett time to deal with Diana.

"I'm sorry, Diana. I can't see it anywhere." I tell her after a few minutes of looking around.

"Oh not to worry. My dog, Benji, he's a Westie, has probably taken it off somewhere."

"I'll walk you out, Mum." Emmett gets up from his seat.

"That won't be necessary." Diana says. "Sarah's perfectly capable of seeing me to the door."

I don't understand why she can't let herself out seeing as she'd let herself in, but I humour her. She kisses the babies goodbye, picking each of them out of the high chairs. Of course, Louis decides he doesn't want putting back in and so she has to pass him to Emmett.

We walk down the hall. "I'm not stupid you

know." Diana says to me. "I'm well aware I can't do everything you can do. You're what? I'd guess over fifty years younger than I am?"

"I'm not trying to take your place, Diana. Emmett has offered me the chance to care for the babies and the house while he's at work, and you'll still be their grandma, able to visit as often as you like."

"I'm well aware of that. I don't need you to tell me so." Her friendly demeanour has slipped. "I'm sure you'll be an asset to the house, but let's get one thing clear. You'll be the hired help. I can and will call around whenever I like." She picks up a photo off the side. I'd not noticed it before, too busy following Emmett through the door. It's a photo of Emmett and his wife, his hand over the bloom of her gently rounded belly. She was beautiful. Dark-haired, dark-eyed and oh so pretty. "Louisa was the lady of this house, and her spirit does and will continue to live on, so that those children in there know they had a mother who loved them. She didn't have any parents of her own and so I swore I would help Emmett keep her memory alive." Tears well up in the old woman's eyes and I reach out for her, but she turns away.

"I'll be off now." She says and she leaves me

standing on the doorstep wondering if I want to be part of this tragic affair after all.

10

EMMETT

"I'm so sorry."

She stills at the sound of my voice but she doesn't move. I shouldn't have been eavesdropping on what my mother was saying to her but after how she acted towards Sarah when she first arrived, I wanted to make sure she was polite. Sarah may have only been here a few hours but already I know I'll be offering her this job. She just fits in our life and the house feels so relaxed with her calm and gentle manner.

Her shoulders visibly tense before she spins but even when she's facing me, she refuses to look up.

"I should probably go." The sadness in her

voice makes something inside me ache. I can't say goodbye to her while she's seems so defeated.

Racking my brain for a reason to keep her here a little longer, I eventually come up with something I hope will work.

"I've never done online shopping before. I was hoping you could help and we could meal plan for the week. That way you'll get to know what I like." It's a total lie and the way her brows draw together tells me that she's instantly suspicious.

"You work in IT. You're more than capable of figuring out an online shopping website and we both know it."

Deciding to show my hand, I forget about the bullshit lies and grow a pair of balls.

"Okay, fine. I'm not ready for you to leave yet."

Her mouth opens and then closes again, clearly changing her mind about the words that formed on her tongue.

"If I'm being honest then you can be too."

"I just..." She hesitates and I worry that she's about to turn down my offer because of my interfering mother. She momentarily glances at the photo of Louisa and I on the sideboard and suddenly her reluctance makes sense.

"She'd want this. She'd want her babies to be looked after by someone so..."

"So?" She prompts when I stumble for the right word.

"Incredible."

Her cheeks heat but she doesn't try to argue this time.

"Where's your computer then? Let's get this show on the road."

We sit side by side on the sofa, me with my laptop, her with a notepad and together we plan the food for the week while her body heat scorches my side and my babies nap upstairs. It feels so normal, so right, and I don't know whether to be happy or panicked about the fact it's her that makes me feel that way.

She seems to forget about the idea of leaving and instead insists that I sit and watch the TV while she finds something to cook for us all. I don't bother changing the channel from the kids one it was on earlier and instead get on the floor with my little monsters and enjoy playing with them without concerns of dinner and responsibilities nagging me.

Sarah rustles up an incredible macaroni cheese. She tries to apologise for its simplicity but it's everything. She's yet to know what a terrible cook I am. I try my best but I'm no Nigella, that's for sure.

I insist on at least filling the dishwasher since she's relieved me of so much today when technically she's not even employed yet.

She relents but only because she uses the time to give the twins their yoghurts.

"I really should get going. Thank you for making me feel so welcome today. I know I've said it before but those two really are a credit to you. You've done an incredible job."

It doesn't matter how many times she tells me, each time my heart still swells with pride for my babies. I know I'm totally biased but they are amazing.

"You sure you don't want to stay for bath time?"

"No, I really should get back before my parents send out a search party. What time would you like me tomorrow?"

"The twins have doctors appointments in the morning. So how about after lunch sometime? We can all have dinner again. If that's okay with you, of course?" I don't want to assume she's okay with cooking for us once again but now I've had a taste of her abilities I don't really want to go back to my own thrown together creations. I'm sure the twins would fully agree if they could.

"That sounds perfect. I'll look forward to it."

"Me too."

Taking her coat from the hook in the hallway, I hold it out for her to slip into and show her to the door.

It feels wrong. That after just a day here, her heading upstairs to the master bedroom I have ready for the nanny I finally decided on would feel so natural.

I bite my tongue from offering her the job because I know she wants to wait until she's in the clear. But I can't lie, it's becoming less and less of an issue for me. I know without a doubt it's a naïve kid's false accusation. I like to think I've met the real Sarah and the person I'm becoming so fond of would never raise a hand to a child.

My house feels cold and empty when I close the door behind her.

Not allowing myself to focus on that, I walk into the living room and scoop up a twin under each arm and head upstairs for bath time. One of our favourite times of the day. I love their little smiles as they splash about without a care in the world.

When I fall asleep later that night, it's with my head full of thoughts I shouldn't allow. Images of Sarah making herself at home here fill my mind. But it's not just her cooking in the kitchen or feeding the twins. It's more than that and for the first time since Louisa died I start to consider the possibility of moving on.

Ash, being the manwhore that he is has mentioned more than once that I need a good shag; even Ross has suggested I consider dating again. I shun the idea every time either bring it up because my life is full enough right now. I didn't think I'd fall in love again after my first disaster of a relationship, but Louisa appeared and I was powerless to do anything but fall for her. When she was also taken away from me, although for very different reasons, I swore I was done. I'd had my heart smashed twice. *So why do I keep seeing Sarah as part of my future? And not just as my babies' nanny?*

THE NEXT THREE days fly by and by the time Sarah rings the doorbell on Friday morning I'm ready to hand her over a key and demand she never leaves.

The twins love her. The smile that spreads across both of their faces every time they see her melts my heart. And I must admit that after just a few days, she's making more of an impression on me than I was anticipating, and I don't just think that's because I'm eating properly again for the first time in a year, or because she seems to do some kind of magic before bedtime. Since she appeared the twins have both slept through the night. I feel like a new man after a few full nights' sleep. It makes me think that I might actually be capable of heading back to work again and be able to function like an adult.

"Good morning," I sing when I pull the door open.

"Wow, did you guys have another good night?"

"Yep, slept right through. I'd forgotten what it feels like to not be exhausted."

"That's awesome. I'm glad I could help. Is there anything specific you'd like me to do today?"

"I don't think so. I've already changed the sheets and put the towels in the wash. I thought that maybe we could go out this afternoon?"

"Of course. I'll just make lunch and prep dinner and we can go wherever you'd like."

She hangs up her coat and slips off her shoes like she belongs here and after saying hello to Elouise and Louis who are busy playing on the living room floor, she heads straight for the kitchen.

I should go back to the twins and leave her to it but the sight of her bending over as she rummages through the fridge catches my eye as I pass and I can't help but stop and stare.

She's wearing a pair of grey skinny jeans with a pink jumper, it's simple and shouldn't be as hot as she's making it look.

My eyes are glued to the spot. I'm totally lost in my own head when she moves and stands up straight. She must feel my stare because she turns to me making my heart skip a beat that I've been caught.

"Sorry, did you say something?"

"I... uh... um... just wondered what was for lunch."

Her smile tells me she doesn't believe a word that's just fallen from my lips, but she humours me anyway. "I was just going to do turkey salad sandwiches. Is that okay?"

"Yeah perfect. I'm starved." I cringe at my words but soon realise that she can't know food isn't really the thing I'm starved for right now.

Giving myself a good talking to, I head into the living room to check on the twins. I want this woman to move in and be a part of our lives as an employee. I need to stop imagining her in a totally different role and sleeping in a totally different bed.

"Food's up," she calls a few minutes later. And after sweeping both my kids up, we head into the kitchen to join her.

"Whoa, this looks good."

"It's just sandwiches." She's right, it is. But it looks a hell of a lot nicer than any sandwich I've ever made for myself.

Once we've eaten, we bundle the twins up into their winter romper suits and head out deciding that we'll take them for a trip to the local farm to see the animals.

"I haven't been here for years," Sarah says when I pull the car into a car park. "I feel like a kid again."

"I used to love it here too. I think I had almost all of my birthday parties here."

"Oh, I might have something in common with

your mum then," she says with a chuckle. I was worried what she'd think after they first met earlier in the week but it seems that Sarah's pushed any concerns about my mother aside and equally, my mum hasn't been around half as much this week as we try to find our feet, which I'm grateful for.

"I'm sure you'll get on fine once she gets used to the idea."

"I've dealt with worse grandmothers I can assure you."

"I'm not sure if I'm happy about that or not." Don't get me wrong, I'm glad my mother isn't the grandmother from hell, but equally, I'm sad that she's had to deal with overbearing grandparents when all she's trying to do is her job.

We strap a child in each before meeting around the back of the double buggy. I don't think much of it and automatically go to grab the handle, but Sarah makes the exact same move and my hands don't wrap around the plastic, but instead the warm skin of her hands.

"Oh, I'm so sorry." I intend on pulling my hands away but when our eyes meet, I'm frozen in place. Her light blue eyes bore into mine. My mouth waters and my heart races as our connection holds. She's been driving me crazy for days and the sudden desire to reach forward and pull her into my body is almost all consuming. Her mouth opens slightly, dragging my eyes from hers and her tongue sneaks out and licks across her bottom lip. My muscles ache to reach out for her and just before I lose the fight, she turns away and pulls her hands from beneath mine.

"What shall we see first then? The donkeys were always my favourite."

"I'm more of an alpaca man myself."

11

SARAH

I've never fancied the man I worked for before.
Thank God.

But something is happening here. I'm finding it
harder to deny it. As we walk around the farm and
I watch Emmett pushing the double buggy, I can't
deny that things that shouldn't be happening in my
knickers area are happening in my knickers area.
It's obviously just a daft crush I've got going on.
Maybe the whole 'tragic Sex God widower who
needs rescuing' is doing it for me?

I'm an idiot.

I don't think it is that though. Truth is, I think
it's just Emmett himself. He's good looking, he's a
great guy, and I am sure he keeps looking at me in a
way that he shouldn't.

Please tell me I am not imagining this.

Oh, Sarah. I plead with myself. Don't do anything to mess this potential job up. You need it. It's your ticket out of hell.

Because that's what life at home with my parents and brother is.

Sheer hell.

I love my niece dearly but not every morning at five am.

I love my brother but not complaining about his girlfriend while he drinks several cans of alcohol, finally leaving the sofa at two am.

My parents are fantastic people, but not when they're moaning about having their house back, although I get it, I really do.

My brother's girlfriend is fine, when she's not in MY room.

I am absolutely exhausted, and I'm surprised that Emmett has not noticed my continual yawning yet.

"Alpacas are growing on me." I tell him, "though I'm still all about the donkeys."

"Neigh, girl. Alpacas hands down."

"Did you just make a really bad dad joke?"

Emmett shrugs his shoulders. God, even that is done sexily. "I am a dad, I'm allowed."

"Hmm."

We wander down to the donkeys and I bend down to feed them while talking to them in a baby voice.

"Nice ass." Emmett states.

What the fuck?

I spin around and Emmett is almost folded double while laughing and pointing at the donkey.

"Oh. OH. Another dad joke."

He can barely breathe for laughing. I stand with my hands folded across my chest.

"Come on. I'll treat you to a coffee and some cake to make up for having to listen to my jokes."

"Ooooh I hope they have cookies!! And I will choose the most expensive as punishment." I smile as we head in the direction of the cafe.

But he doesn't stop there. I'm ordering a double chocolate chip cookie when he points to a cake. "Thought you wanted the most expensive?"

"This is the most expensive." My brow furrows.

"No that's Madeira cake. My dearer cake. Get it?" He's off again.

"Seriously, Emmett, have you been drinking today?"

He holds his cheeks. "Oh God, my face is

cramping. Sorry, Sarah. I'm just having fun and my god has it been a long time since I did."

"Fine. You may carry on with the jokes, but I'm having two cookies now."

I polish off both cookies and rub my stomach. Emmett stares at my plate. "How are you so slim?"

I shrug. "Young metabolism. Anyway, you're not exactly fat, are you?"

"Running around after twins and a home gym. It's hiding in a shed in the garden."

"Ah."

"You can use it if you like?"

"Are you saying I need to shape up?" I quip.

"Gosh, no, you have an amazing figure." He trails off. "I'm making this worse. My mouth just needs taping up before it says anything else to embarrass me."

"Hey for an old man, you're not so bad yourself." Eloise babbles. "Yes, you have a lovely daddy, don't you?" I coo.

My phone begins to ring.

Reaching into my bag, I bring it out. Number not recognised.

"Hello?"

"Hello there. Is that Sarah Fletcher?"

"It is."

"It's PC Marlow here."

My body tenses and I feel the blood drain from my face. My heart thuds.

Emmett must notice because he comes closer to me. "What's wrong?"

I shake my head at him.

"Just to let you know that Melinda has confessed to making the whole thing up. The family are extremely sorry for what's occurred. I think they will try to reach out to you. I advised them that it might be best that they just leave things alone. Anyway, you're completely in the clear and our investigation is now completed. We've had a word with the young lady about wasting police time."

My shoulders sag in relief and my eyes fill with tears.

"Thank you so much. Thank you for calling me. For everything."

"You're welcome. I hope you find a nice new family to look after."

"I think I already have." I state.

I put my phone down on the table. "That was the police. Melinda has confessed to lying. The case is closed. I'm free." I break out into a relieved smile.

Emmett's hand clasps mine. This time I don't pull away from him.

"Then can you eat another cookie because we need to celebrate?"

"No, but another coffee would be nice."

"Coming right up."

He brings hot drinks to the table, placing them well away from the infants' reach.

"So, Sarah." He takes a deep breath. "Would you like the job of nanny with us, and can you move in as soon as possible?"

"Yes. I'd love that." My day is getting better and better. "I can't wait to start work. And to get some sleep."

"Sleep with twins? Good luck with that one."

I explain how I've been existing on three hours sleep a night.

"Okay. Well, let's go and get your things. Then tonight we'll have a takeaway to celebrate your new role and then you can have a good night's sleep. I'll see to my babies. We'll carry on finding our way into who's going to do what for the next week and then a week on Monday you're on your own because I have to go back to work."

"Okay. How about this next week we take it in

turns to get up with the twins, so we get a good night's sleep every other night?"

Emmett picks up his coffee mug. "I'll say cheers to that."

I raise mine and clink it with his.

"I think we should celebrate with a bottle of wine tonight." Emmett adds.

I give him a wary look.

"If we only have one each, we should manage to not have hangovers, right?"

"Okay, just one, because I don't want to lose my job before it starts because I'm off my face."

"Well, your official start date is tomorrow, just in case." Emmett laughs.

"I'll just be having the one." I insist.

I WALK into my house with Emmett following behind.

"Emmett!" My mum shouts almost deafening the man. "So good to see you. Oh, where are the little ones?"

"They're with my mum right now. You'll have to pop by some time to see them." He tells her, accepting her hug.

"So what are you doing here?"

"I've come to steal your daughter." He laughs.

Luke walks in as Emmett speaks. "You got yourself a sugar daddy? Good one, sis." He winks.

"Luke!" My mum admonishes him. "It's Emmett from Dad's work, you idiot."

Luke's face pales. "Oh God, I'm so sorry. Erm, how are you stealing Sarah then?"

"She's going to be my new live-in nanny." Emmett announces.

My mum squeals. "Oh that's fantastic news."

"You know she hits kids, right?" My brother announces. I've had enough and I punch him straight in the gut until he doubles over.

"I got cleared, Mum. The police dropped the investigation. The kid admitted they lied."

Mum hugs me. "Oh I'm so pleased, although I didn't for a moment believe you capable of any such thing."

Luke points to his gut while his face remains in a grimace.

"So can I get you anything? Cup of tea?"

"Cuppa would be great." Emmett says. "We're here to get Sarah's things. So that's one less kid under your feet."

Kid. Now I'm the one who feels like I've been punched in the gut.

"Sure you can't take them both?" Mum laughs. While they carry on chatting, I make my excuses and go to get my things from the living room.

KID.

Kid.

Kid.

I can't help feeling gutted. He's employing me to look after his children. Surely that's not how he sees me? But I guess to him I'm young. Come on, Sarah, time to be happy that you have new employment and a new massive bedroom with its own en suite. I remind myself. Then I start loading my belongings into Emmett's car while he chats a little more with my mum. He's comfortable amongst his own age group. I see myself now for what I must look like to him. It's good those boundaries are clear to me, because I'm the nanny anyway. It might stop my ridiculous crush now.

IT TAKES a while but eventually we get back to Emmett's and I get my things put in my new room. I unpack some basics. Everything else can wait until I've had more sleep. Emmett insisted on ordering some Chinese food for half-past eight and has just settled the twins down. I have some suggestions on how to get them to sleep faster but they can wait. I'm going to eat my food, and then politely excuse myself because I feel half dead.

The food arrives and Emmett suggests we eat in the living room, so we sit on the floor, (not a problem due to a lovely thick pile carpet), and he uncorks the wine.

"I'm not sure wine's a good idea. I'm really tired," I tell him.

"But we have to celebrate. No prosecution and a new job," he protests.

"Okay. Just the one then," I tell him and he fills my glass.

We eat the food and chat and I can feel myself start to unwind. The simple fact is that I have a room of my own to go to. I'm not under suspicion of hitting a child anymore. That whole weight just lifts off me. The wine tastes delicious and so when Emmett offers another I say yes.

"I have to say." Emmett states. "That though I'm pleased you're here for my children, I'm just as pleased that you're here for me too."

"Lazy sod. Just want treating like a prince do you?"

"No, I don't mean that. I mean having the company. It's been a long time since I got to chat with someone normally. It's either my mum fussing or babies babbling."

"You have my dad."

"It's not the same. I'm enjoying your company. An educated and fun female perspective."

"Really? Even though I'm just a kid."

Oh dear. Two glasses of wine and my tongue is looser than a whore's vagina.

"What are you talking about?" Emmett actually looks confused.

"You said to my mum earlier that I would be one less kid under her feet."

His eyes widen. "Yes, in terms of your mum. You are a kid to your mum. Mine will still be my kids even when they're all grown up." He laughs, but I can't interpret what kind of laugh it is.

"I think I'd better go to bed," I state.

"I don't see you as a kid, Sarah," Emmett says. "In fact, what I see you as, well, it could ruin everything."

My head snaps back to his.

"What are you saying?" I ask, although part of my mind is screaming for me to just leave the room before he speaks.

"I'm saying it's been a long, long time since I took a woman to my bed, but right now I just want to fuck you, Sarah. Still think I see you as a kid now?"

I swallow slowly and take a deep breath.

"What are you waiting for then?" I push.

"My mind is trying to tell me you're my employee. My body is telling me you're a beautiful woman."

You can hear only our breathing in the otherwise silent room.

"I don't start work until tomorrow."

The air between us crackles but neither of us moves. His eyes drop from mine and instead focus on my lips. Without instruction from my brain, my tongue sneaks out and wets my bottom one before my teeth sink into it. I want to feel his lips pressed up against mine so fucking badly. I want to know if they're as soft as I imagine they are. I want to know if he can kiss as expertly as I expect him to.

My heart pounds; I feel it in every single part of my body as the silence stretches between us.

I can't help thinking he's daring me. Daring me not to move, not to run from this. If that's the case, then he clearly doesn't know me all that well yet because I'm not one to back down. Especially if it's something I want just as badly.

I know this shouldn't be happening. I know that I should put a stop to it right now, but I fear that under his intense stare I'm powerless to do anything but follow his lead.

"Fuck, Sarah." He closes the space between us, his hands resting on the carpet either side of my hips, forcing me to lean back just slightly.

His eyes drop lower and I've no doubt he can see straight down the front of my jumper at this angle. He can see how much my chest is heaving and how much he's affecting me. If he goes lower, he'll no doubt see my nipples trying to break free from the fabric and there'll be no questioning what it is I want right now.

His lips. His hands. His cock. His everything.

"Emmett." It's meant to be a question, but it comes out more like a breathy moan. It does the job because his resistance snaps.

He closes the space between us. My breasts brush up against his chest sending sparks of lust shooting off around my body before his hand cups my cheek and slides around into my hair so he can pull my lips to his.

He's gentle for the first two seconds, but then

he crushes his lips to mine and I've no choice to lie back as he crawls over me. I moan as his tongue slips past my lips and mine eagerly joins in the intimate dance he initiates.

Time to show him just how much of a grown woman I am.

12

EMMETT

My lips are no more than a centimetre from hers. Her soft breaths caress across my face. I shouldn't be doing this. I should get up right now and walk to my bedroom like I never admitted I wanted to fuck her. But, shit if that's not exactly what I want to do right now.

She's been sitting beside me, her sweet, floral scent filling my nose for the past hour and the only thing I can think about is having my hands on her body. Her curves are so fucking sexy and I already know from last Saturday night that our bodies would line up perfectly. That thought alone has my cock pressing against my zip trying to break free to get to her.

I'm holding on to my last thread of restraint

when she moans my name. It's no more than a soft plea on her lips but it's the final straw.

I've moved without realising and before I know it, she's on her back, her lips against mine and she's exploring my mouth.

Holy fuck, this is happening.

Unable to keep my hands to myself, especially now that she could freak out at any moment and pull away, I drop my hand from her hair in favour of her breast.

She moans and arches her back as I gently squeeze. The moan that rumbles up her throat almost has me coming on the damn spot.

It's been too damn long.

Needing to hear those noises again, I find the hem of her jumper and slip my hand inside. The hot, smooth skin of her stomach is addictive as I trail my fingertips up until I find the lace that's covering her.

Finding her peaked nipple, I pinch it with my thumb and forefingers and she damn near purrs with pleasure.

This woman's going to be the death of me and we're both still fully dressed.

My lungs burn with my need for air. I reluctantly pull my lips from hers, but unable to remove them from her, I trail light kisses across her jaw and down her neck.

"Emmett, oh, oh, please."

"Please what?" I moan into the sensitive skin of her neck.

"Please, I need..." Sitting up slightly, I push the fabric of her jumper up over her breast to reveal her white lace bra. Her dusky pink nipples are visible beneath the sheer fabric and my mouth waters for a taste.

"You need?" I ask, trailing my finger gently along the edge of the lace, enjoying watching her squirm beneath me.

"You. Everything. Now," her chest heaves beneath my touch telling me that she means every single word.

"What kind of man would I be to deny you that?" I lift my gaze to her face and my breath catches at the sight of her dark, almost black eyes.

Taking hold of the fabric once again, I pull it up and over her head. The move makes her dark hair fan out on the cream carpet.

I drop my lips back to her lips, unable to resist her, but I don't linger long this time. I've got more to explore.

I trail kisses down her neck, along her collarbone and down her chest.

"Oh God," she moans, the closer I get to her breasts. "Emmett, please. I need... I need..."

Her demands are cut off when I pull one of her bra cups down to expose her swollen breast.

"So fucking perfect."

"Fuuuuck," she cries as I suck her nipple into my mouth. Her back leaves the floor as she offers more of herself to me.

Fuck. This woman.

She moans and writhes to the point I think she's going to come from this alone. I smile to myself that she was clearly sitting there just as worked up as I was.

Pulling the fabric down on the other side I give it the same treatment and she curses and begs for more.

Needing to commit this image to memory before she becomes my employee and that the possibility of this ever happening again is too much, I sit up and look down at her, and fuck if it's not the best sight I've ever seen.

Reaching behind me, I pull my shirt over my head and drop it somewhere near where I threw hers not so long ago.

Her eyes immediately drop to my chest, her teeth attacking her bottom lip as she takes her fill. I can't deny that it's not a huge boost to my ego that someone as stunning and young as her still looks at my half naked body with hunger and need pouring from her eyes.

Not waiting to find out if she's going to do or say anything, I drop my lips back to her skin. I'm addicted to her taste already and I don't think I'm going to be sated until I've had every single fucking inch of her.

Popping the button on the waistband of her jeans, she lifts her hips to help me shimmy them off of her. Once they're free of her body and with the small pile we're starting, she sits herself up and lifts her arms behind her back. One quick flick of her fingers and her bra falls away from her body.

"Fuck. I need you naked right fucking now."

While she takes care of her top half, I focus my attention on the bottom but I'm nowhere near as careful as she was as I wrap my fingers around the sides and tug until the satisfying sound of the fabric ripping fills the room.

"Oh my god, you didn't?" Her eyes fly down to the ruined lace in my hands. "That's so fucking hot."

She falls back onto her elbows and watches my journey as I kiss down her stomach, circle her belly button with my tongue and then descend towards where we both need me to be if her whimpers of need are anything to go by.

The scent of her sweetness fills my nose long before I get to my final prize. My cock weeps to be released but it's not my turn yet. This isn't about me. This is about Sarah and giving her what she needs. Plus, I somewhat selfishly want to watch her coming almost more than I want to find my release myself.

Parting her lips, my tongue darts out to find her clit. She cries out when I make contact. Her thighs squeeze my head with an incredible force. Pressing my palms against the inside of her legs, I spread her as wide as she'll go, not taking my eyes from her for a second. She's totally bare and fucking stunning; it's all I can do not to take her right this second. Just imagining how she'll look when she's stretched open has my balls drawing up in preparation.

"Fuck, you're beautiful."

"Emmett." It's the first time she's sounded hesitant and when I look up at her, I find a deep blush on her cheeks and down onto her neck.

"You've got nothing to be embarrassed about,

baby. This is the thing dreams are fucking made of." I run my finger down the length of her and she bucks from the floor. "Don't scream too loud," I warn before diving back down and sucking her clit into my mouth.

Her hands thread into my hair and as I up my tempo, her grip gets tighter, ensuring I'm not able to stop.

"Hmmm," I moan against her when I sense she's getting close to the edge.

"Oh God, oh fuck. Emmett. Shiiiit. Fuuuuck."

Her body tenses before she cries my name and gives into the pleasure. Her hips rock as she rides my face, finding every single last second of her pleasure.

Sitting up, I wipe my face with the back of my hand and stare down at her exhausted and sated body.

"You finished? I ask, praying to whoever might be listening that she doesn't say yes.

Her eyes pop open, giving me a shot at the glassy orbs beneath. Fuck, she looks unbelievable.

Her eyes drop from mine and run down my chest until she finds the very obvious bulge in my jeans.

"I think we're anywhere but finished, don't you?"

"Fucking right."

Reaching over, I quickly slosh the last of the wine into a glass and take a swig.

"Want some?"

She nods and I'm about to hand her the glass before I have a better idea. Taking another sip, I lean back over her and place my lips to hers. She figures out what I'm doing and opens hers slightly.

Some of it goes into her mouth but a generous amount trickles down the side of her face, allowing me to trail my lips along and lick it from her skin. I've never tasted something so fucking sweet.

It's only the feeling of her fingers at my waistband that stops me. I still, my muscles freezing, knowing that for the first time in fuck knows how long I'm about to be touched by a woman. It feels like it's been an eternity. I may as well be a fifteen-year-old boy again for how excited I am. And also like a hormone filled teenager I'm worried that I'll go off the second she makes any kind of contact with me.

"Sarah, fuck," I moan when she opens up the fabric and pushes her hand inside my boxers. She grasps me tightly and my hips thrust forward needing so much more than just her touch. Heat turns from where she's holding me and threatens to turn me into a puddle of fucking lava.

Jumping up from her, I make quick work of removing my remaining clothing. I'm just about to crawl back on top of her when the feeling of her soft lips against my thighs stops me.

Looking down, I find her on her knees before me. My cock jutting out, twitching, hoping for some action as she slowly makes her way towards him.

Holy shit, how am I going to last with her like that?

"I'll take it slow."

Fuck. Did I just say that out loud?

My head falls back, mortified by admitting how close to the wire I am already but the second her tiny hand wraps around me once again I'm powerless but to watch as she slowly works me up and down.

The soft, gentleness of her touch has nothing on my hand and I fear she's just ruined hand jobs for me forever now.

After a couple of strokes, she leans forward, her tongue sneaking out to lick at the tip.

"Fuck me."

"That's the plan." The wicked smile she graces me with almost has me on my knees.

She doesn't allow me to respond, even if I did have something to come back with because her hand slips down my length and she sucks me deep into her hot mouth.

"Fuuuuuuck." My hands find her hair and I gently guide her to stop her going too fast and putting an end to this before it's even really begun.

She sucks, licks, pumps, and squeezes my balls. Each action dragging me closer to the earth-shattering release that I know is to come.

"Sarah, I'm... I'm..." I try to warn her that I'm about to explode, but the pleasure is so intense that I can't get my brain to function enough to muster up the words. Instead I tap the top of her head, desperate for her to know what's about to happen so she can make an informed decision as to how she'd like to finish it.

She doesn't pull back. She doesn't even fucking hesitate. And it's then that I know I've got a serious fucking problem on my hands.

"Sarah," I roar, my hands fisting her hair as my cock twitches and my cum fills her mouth. She takes it all, no hesitation, and when she pulls back and wipes her mouth, she's got the smuggest fucking grin on her face.

Pulling her to her feet, I slam my lips to hers and lift her into my arms. I'm done with the living room fucking floor. If I'm going to fuck her properly it's going to be on a bed when I can get her good and comfortable for the ride.

13

SARAH

I know this is a bad idea.

But then why does it feel so good?

Right now I refuse to think about tomorrow, about anything other than the incredible feelings coursing through my body courtesy of this amazing man.

There's something about him. Maybe it is the fact he's older, but I don't feel shy, or nervous. Instead, I feel like I can truly be a woman with him, ask for what I want, take what I need, do what I like.

And he seems to be enjoying what I've been doing so far if his heady moans when he came down my throat were any indication.

I'm so wet right now. I can feel it at the top of

my thighs. Emmett is carrying me up the stairs like I'm a bag of air. This is totally crazy. My first night in this house and I'm headed to a different room than the one I'm supposed to be in.

He kicks open his bedroom door, walks in and places me gently on his bed, the mattress depressing as he climbs on with me. The room smells of Emmett, all spicy notes. As he reaches forward to kiss me once more, I take in a deep inhale of him. The mix of spice and wine. I think I'm drunk on Emmett alone.

"Did you just smell me?" Emmett chuckles as he trails his lips up my throat.

"Yes." I admit. "You smell so fucking good."

"You taste so fucking good." Emmett moans, his lips trailing across my collarbone, down the curve of my breast, across my stomach. He moves to my feet and kisses up one leg and then the other until he reaches the top of each thigh and then he leaves me bereft and this time moves and picks up my arm, kissing from my wrist up past my elbow.

"Emmett, please." I'm desperate now for his touch.

"Please what?"

"Please fuck me."

His fingers tease at my entrance, trailing up my

seam and pushing inside. "So fucking wet for me."
He groans as I buck to meet the thrust of his digits.

"Come on my fingers." He urges, setting a
rhythm to his digits pumping inside me. I lean up
and pull his head towards mine so that our mouths
clash together and as I come hard, he swallows my
moans with his mouth.

I'm panting, now laid back against the pillow.
"Do you have condoms?"

"Yeah." He smiles. "My best friend Ash bought
me a whole box full a month ago. Let me go grab a
couple." He looks almost shy for a moment. "I
wasn't expecting to need one tonight."

I watch as he gets off the bed and pads over to
his wardrobe. That taut fine arse of his is a joy to
behold, along with the muscles in his thighs and
calves.

When he turns back around he catches me
perving, but my mouth goes dry because Emmett
has a huge cock, erect, and looking like it means
business.

"Were you staring at my butt?" Emmett raises a
brow. I watch as he sheathes his dick in a condom.

"Oh yeah, and now I'm staring at your cock.
Hurry up, I'm going hungry over here."

He strolls, the bastard. Taking his damn time.

Eventually, after what seems like forever he gets back on the bed and moves over me.

"Are you ready for me, Sarah?"

The tip of his cock nudges at my entrance.

I moan. "I'm so, so ready."

He angles his hips and pushes inside me slowly. I feel him slip into me, the feeling of fullness so fucking divine. I moan and clasp his backside with my hands.

"Ohhh."

He pulls back. "Look at me, Sarah."

I open my eyes and stare directly into his as he pushes inside me yet again. "God, you feel so fucking amazing. So tight."

He keeps moving so slowly and I feel like I'm going to go insane with need and then he starts increasing his pace and his thrusts become more fervent. I see a sheen of sweat on his brow and as my eyes close once more and our movements become more frenzied, I feel a droplet splash my chest.

Emmett's moves are now causing my head to just slightly bang into the headboard and I don't give a damn as I feel myself climbing towards my release. He stills for a moment and then pumps inside me once, twice, three times, and the third time takes me over, my walls pulsing around him milking him for every last drop.

He gathers me in his arms and pulls me close and I open my eyes to look at the guy who just gave me more pleasure in one night than any of my previous boyfriends did added together. But then I realise that it wasn't a bead of sweat that hit my chest, but a tear.

Because Emmett has several more of them coursing down his cheek.

What the fuck have we done?

"EMMETT?" I pull him closer. "I'm sorry. I'm so sorry."

"No." He says firmly. "You don't understand." He wipes his face. "I'm not upset. It's relief." He strokes my hair. "This was always going to be a big deal. My first time with someone else, someone who's not my wife. It couldn't have been better, Sarah. In fact, it was fucking amazing."

"You're not just saying that so I don't feel bad?" I question.

"No, I'm not just saying that." He reassures me. "And give me a minute and then I'm going to show you yet again just how much I don't regret it."

And he does, several times.

We fall asleep in each other's arms. The next thing I know, it's morning. The daylight from the slightly open curtain is waking me up, and the space at the side of me is empty and cold.

It's strange getting out of the bed I shouldn't be in. Walking into my own room, I stare at the still made bed, not a wrinkle on the quilt or an indent on the pillow. Grabbing the towels Emmett had left on the end of it, I go straight into the shower and wash the smell of sex from my body. I'm not sure what to expect today. We said that last night I wasn't an employee. Today I am. And so even though it seems entirely weird to act as if last night never happened, that's what I intend to do, because my focus needs to be on these children now and in making sure Emmett feels confident enough to leave me to look after them while he returns to work and to a more usual life. I don't regret what happened between us for a second, but I recognise it for what it was. Two people finding each other attractive, taking what they needed. Now somehow, I have to put a barrier up between that Emmett and Sarah, the man and the woman; and make sure Emmett and Sarah, employer and employee appear.

After showering and drying my hair and body, I dress in a simple pair of navy bootcut trousers and a grey polo neck. Then I head downstairs into the kitchen where Emmett is busy feeding the twins porridge. There is more on their faces and bodies than I reckon they've eaten. As he spoons an extra mouthful to Elouise, Louis takes the opportunity to put his hand in his bowl and rub it in his cheeks and then he giggles at me.

"Having fun?" I ask Emmett.

"I think they might need a bath somehow." He looks at me in despair. "I didn't want to wake you because I promised you a lie in, but please can you finish feeding Louis while there's food left to give him?"

I pick up the bowl and spoon and hold it to Louis' mouth and he opens wide to eat it.

"Good boy." I stroke his messy porridge riddled cheek. He smiles at me, displaying a mouth full of food before swallowing it down.

He eats up the rest of his food greedily and I grab the baby wipes from the countertop, wipe his face and hands and then clean up the tray. Emmett finishes feeding Elouise and I do the same with her.

"Quick change of tops and they won't need a

bath just yet. I'm sure they've not finished messing themselves up yet." I reach for the kettle. "Now go sit in the living room, and I don't know, look at the morning news or *Saturday Kitchen* or something, while I make us drinks and some breakfast."

"I can do that." He rises from his seat.

"This is my first day working isn't it?" I place my hands on my hips. "So let me get to it and go and relax. You've been up early."

"Several times." He states, then he places a hand over his eyes. "I mean with the twins. They woke several times in the night."

I laugh. "You should have woken me."

He shrugs. "You looked so peaceful and I promised you a lie in."

"Well, if you want to go back to bed after breakfast, I have here covered."

"I think I'm going to love having you here, Sarah." He says, and then he leaves the kitchen, leaving me a confused bag of emotions.

"Right, kiddiwinkles." I turn to the twins. "What shall I make me and Daddy for breakfast before I get you in your buggy and take you for some lovely fresh air around the park?"

After eating some toast and swallowing coffee, I take a cooked breakfast through to Emmett. I put some washing in the machine and then make sure the changing bag has everything I need. I find the twins' coats hung at the bottom of the stairs along with their shoes and get them ready. Just before I place the buggy outside the door and put the twins in it, I go through to Emmett.

"We're off to the park."

He leaps up. "Oh, give me a minute. I'll come with you."

I shake my head. "No need. Go get that sleep you can have now."

He stands and I see the conflicting emotions cross his face. He doesn't know whether he wants to leave them. Finally, he takes a deep breath. "That'll be nice. Have a good time at the park. Here, I'll help you get them in the buggy."

All wrapped up and after he's checked with me that I have everything, he kisses his babies and waves us off down the driveway. We wave back and then turn the corner for the park, leaving Daddy on the doorstep. I don't think for a minute he'll manage to sleep. He'll be waiting for the second my key turns in the lock to know his kids are back safely, but one day soon he'll get there. I know that, because I've seen it before, and it's my job to make sure he feels secure enough to go to work and not worry about his children while he's gone.

While I'm in the park, I sit on a bench for a moment. It's a crisp but quite mild day and I pull my phone out of my bag and call Reese.

"Hey. You okay to talk?" I always ask this given she has a young baby.

"I am. Bree's asleep. I was just thinking about you, funnily enough."

"You were. Why?"

"All in good time. Why are you calling me first?"

"Well, mainly to tell you that the police dropped their investigation. The little twat confessed to lying."

"Oh thank fuck for that, Sarah. You must be so relieved."

"I am, and that's not all. Emmett offered me the childcare job straightaway after we found out, helped me get my things from my parents' house and I've started today."

"Wow, that's incredible... and... super-fast."

"Well, I needed out of my house and I needed a job."

"Sure this Emmett isn't wanting more than a nanny?"

"Don't be silly." I feel the hairs on the back of my neck stand up because my friend is too close to the truth for comfort. "He's just desperate to get a routine sorted before he goes back to work a week on Monday."

"Okay. Calm down. Anyway, that's fantastic news. All clear and with a new job and a room not at your parents' house."

"Huh, might not have been so bad if I'd had a room and not the bloody sofa."

"Nah, Luke would still be there."

"Yeah, true. So, spill, why was I on your mind?"

"Because I spoke to Kaylie last night, and Scott had called her. He asked her to find a way to give you his number."

"Are you fucking kidding me?" I shout down the phone.

"Hey, calm down. Don't shoot the messenger."

"Sorry. But you can rip his number up. I don't want it."

"Apparently he wants to apologise to you. I'll keep the number for now. Think about it. Maybe you could clear the air and then be able to move on from the one we're not allowed to talk about."

"Who we are currently talking about."

"That's the last I'll say about it, other than to reiterate that I will keep the number just in case. Now tell me more about these babies. Are they going to enjoy a visit sometime from a baby girl called Bree?"

And with that all talk of Scott is dropped and talk of Emmett avoided.

14

EMMETT

I feel lost the second she closes the front door behind them. I tell myself that it's because she's taking my babies, but I know it's more than that. Mum's taken them out without me more times than I can count; it's not unusual. This empty feeling in the pit of my stomach is because *she* just left. And she just left after saying absolutely nothing about what happened between us last night.

Secretly, I was glad when I heard the twins stirring and it allowed me to roll out of bed while she was still fast asleep. My head was a mess. Not only did I sleep with my nanny before she'd even officially started the job, but I fucking cried like a pussy afterwards.

I didn't have any intention of showing her

quite how much emotion she dragged up, but the second she fell apart beneath me, I couldn't contain it.

It's been a long year since there was a woman in my bed, since I had my hands on a woman. I thought I'd dealt with the fact I was set for living a life of celibacy, but one taste of her sweetness and I lost my goddamn mind.

I blame her. If she wasn't so... so fucking incredible then it might not have hit me so hard. But she was everything. She was confident, she knew what she wanted, and she wasn't ashamed to get exactly that. Age didn't matter, our roles in life didn't matter. Nothing mattered and that was one scary fucking thought.

I wander around the house wondering what to do while I'm alone and I soon find myself leaning against the doorframe to my bedroom staring at my bed as images from last night play out in front of my eyes.

Until the night I came home without my wife, this room was no more than a storage room. It's slightly bigger than the twins' room and we almost set the nursery up here, but knowing it was farther from our bedroom we changed our mind, needing our babies as close to us as possible. But without her lying beside me, I knew I wouldn't ever be able to get back into our bed ever again.

I slept on the floor that night with the twins' Moses baskets laying side by side next to me. I couldn't even bear to get my clothes out of our room in those first few days. The memories of her; her lingering scent, the sight of her clothes in the wardrobe and her make-up sitting on the dressing table.

A lump crawls up my throat just thinking about how heartbroken I was in those first few weeks without her. I wouldn't wish that kind of pain on my worst enemy. Thank fuck the twins both came out of it without any lasting damage. I'm not sure how I would have continued if I'd lost them as well. As it was they spent a few days in special baby care as they were preemie but they were both perfect and were soon released with a full bill of health to a terrified and broken father.

Falling down on the edge of my bed, I wonder how I managed to get through it all. I think my sleepless nights now are hard; it's so easy to forget the total exhaustion I felt back then.

Knowing that I won't be able to sleep, I pull my shirt over my head and drop my trousers before heading for a long, hot, and uninterrupted shower.

I want to say that I feel like a new man when I eventually step out from under the powerful spray, but I'd be lying. I spent the whole time standing there imagining what it would be like to have Sarah in here with me. To watch the water run over her breasts and down her stomach. I pictured where I might place her as I bent her over, where she might place her hands against the tiles for support as I took her from behind.

Needless to say, I was even more worked up when I wrapped the towel around myself than I was before I got in.

With the towel securely tucked around my waist, I head downstairs for another coffee. The effects of my early morning are really starting to kick in. I figure I can drink and then have a lie down. I may as well make the most of the peace but just as I'm picking up my mug to go back upstairs out of the way a key slides into the lock.

It'll just be Mum coming to interfere with Sarah, I tell myself, but I already know it's not true.

She grunts quietly as she attempts to get the buggy into the house. It fits... just. It was one of the things I researched before we made our choice.

Poking my head into the hallway, I watch as

she backs into the house trying to not jostle what I assume are two sleeping one-year-olds.

She's clearly not expecting to find me watching her because when she turns around she lets out a little shriek, her hand coming up to cover her racing heart.

"Fuck, Emmett. You could have warned me." Halfway through, she must realise I'm not actually wearing any clothes because her eyes drop to take in my still damp chest. My cock swells under her gaze to the point I'm worrying I'm going to be tenting the towel any minute.

"Sorry, I was... uh... going to help."

"I'm pretty sure you shouldn't be going anywhere near the front door dressed like that."

"Why? Worried the woman over the road might want a taste?"

Her eyes narrow and her whole demeanour changes before my eyes.

"About last night," she starts, looking away from my eyes as if she's unable to face what happened between us. It's unnerving seeing her so unsure of herself after her confidence between the sheets—or on top of them.

"Sarah," I whisper, stepping forward and

lifting my hand towards her face. That is until she jumps back.

"No," she snaps. "Last night didn't happen. If this is going to work, then we need to forget about it. You're my employer and I'm your nanny. That's it. That's as far as our relationship can go."

She goes to storm past me and I've no choice but to move aside and let her.

"What if I can't forget?" I ask, although I've no idea if she's escaped far enough to be unable to hear me.

The sound of her bedroom door shutting sounds out and after checking on the twins who are sleeping soundly in their buggy, I also make my way upstairs so I can put on some damn clothes.

When I get there, my phone is lit up on the bedside table. Picking it up, I find a message from Ross.

You. Me. Beer. Pub. 8PM.

SUCCINCT AND TO THE POINT. I can't help smiling. For someone who spends his days working with technology, he's never quite got the hang of texting.

I'll be there.

I'LL CHECK with Sarah if it's okay, but I get the impression that she'll probably be glad to have me out of her hair if our interaction a few minutes ago is anything to go by.

SHE ENDS up leaving the safety of her room before I do. I keep myself locked away, watching reruns of *Top Gear* on the TV to give her some space and to allow her some one-on-one time with the twins. I can hear them giggling over the TV, so I know they're having a great time down there with her.

She calls me down once she has lunch prepared, and with a large sigh, I climb from the bed and head down to see what she's made.

Homemade pizzas greet me when I turn into the kitchen, the smell of the melted cheese and tomatoes making my stomach growl despite the fact she made me a huge fry up this morning.

The twins are busy munching away on a pizza finger when I sit down beside her.

"I'm sorry about earlier. I really don't want things to be awkward between us. I realise that probably wasn't the best way to go about it."

"You don't need to apologise. That wasn't exactly how I was intending on welcoming our new nanny to the house but it's too late now. The deed is done. We'll just take each day as it comes and find a way to ignore it if that's what you want." A part of me dies inside as I say the words because ignoring how she made me feel last night is going to be really fucking hard.

"Good. That's... good."

An awkward silence descends over us and I hate that things have changed between us. That was certainly not my intention. She's the only person I've found that I feel comfortable leaving my babies with and I fear I've screwed it up before it's even really started.

"I'm going out with your dad tonight, so you have the house to yourself."

"Really?" Her face lights up like I've just told her she's won the lottery.

"Yeah. Will you be okay?"

"Are you kidding? A house to myself, well, with the twins of course, is more than okay. I can laze on the sofa and watch the TV without any distractions. It sounds perfect."

"You know that you don't need to work weekends, right?" I ask when she gets up to start washing up. "I'll be home so feel free to do whatever girls your age do at weekends." I cringe the moment the words pass my lips. *Wrong thing to say, dickhead.*

"To be honest, I don't know what *girls my age* do because I've been living in the middle of nowhere for the last... well, it felt like forever. Going out last weekend was the first time in years."

"Okay, well, I just wanted you to know that you're free to do whatever on weekends, just give me a little warning."

"Sure thing, Boss." At no point does she look like she's going to stop cleaning up, so I take the twins into the living room and leave her to it.

"I WON'T BE LATE." She looks up at me from her spot on the sofa and does a quick double take. I can't lie, it does my ego some good even if she's trying to appear totally unaffected by my presence. I haven't really dressed up. I'm only wearing a dark grey shirt and a pair of jeans, but apparently she likes what she sees if the darkening of her eyes is anything to go by.

"Be as late as you like. And if you pull... just keep the noise down, yeah?"

"Sarah, I'm not going—"

"Don't go there, Emmett. We're forgetting it, remember? You going out and meeting a woman *your own age*," she adds with a cringe, "is what you should be doing. I can assure you though that while I'm under your roof, I'll do my... *activities* elsewhere."

Jealousy explodes in my stomach. She's not seriously suggesting that... *no, don't even go there. She's not yours and you have no right to have a say in what she does.*

"I... uh... appreciate that."

"I might see you later then."

With one final look at her, I make my way from the house. The twins are both already fast asleep. I've no clue how she's done it, but I need to get her secrets out of her.

I suck in a lungful of bitter, winter air when I step from the house and try to push aside the feelings she drags up within me. I'm about to spend the evening with her father. I don't need to be thinking about how good his daughter was in the sack last night.

He'll fucking kill you if he ever finds out, a little voice shouts at me, but I push it aside. He won't ever find out because she seems pretty set on it not happening again.

ROSS IS ALREADY SITTING at a table with two pints in front of him when I arrive at our regular.

"I'm glad she let you out to play," he says with a wink as I drop down onto the seat opposite him.

"She's my nanny, not my keeper."

"I know but Sarah has this way of winding people around her little finger. Just you wait, she'll have you exactly where she wants you."

"She's not like that. She's very professional." I want to laugh at that statement. I've known her just over a week and in that time I've seen her blind drunk and fucked her senseless. Very professional.

"I'm sure she is. She's a good girl. Anyway, enough about my brat. I've got you a date."

"You've got me a what?" *Oh shit, no.*

"Date. You remember what one of those is right?"

"Fuck you."

"Nah, you're all right. But you might be thanking me when you meet Celia."

"Celia?" *What kind of name is that?*

"Yeah. She's a looker. She's one of Marie's best friends. Split up with her cheating husband not so long ago and is back on the market. I promise you that you won't regret it. The stories I've heard about that one. Apparently, with one boyfriend she—"

"I don't want to know," I say before he can say something he can't take back.

"Okay, well Marie has arranged a double date for us all on Friday night."

"A double date. Please tell me you're making this shit up."

"I kid you not, mate. I kid you not." He chuckles at the horrified look on my face. I, however, don't see the amusement.

15

SARAH

Emmett has gone out with my dad and instead of enjoying myself in this home I have all to myself tonight apart from two sleeping babies, instead I find myself pummelling the sofa cushions.

"Goddamn it."

I sigh heavily. It's for the best. I know this. Emmett and I need to move along, both date other people our own age. Why did the sex have to be so good? Why does he have to be so hot? Why so nice?

However, it's clear by the fact he keeps bringing the issue up that he still thinks I'm a child. So young. I need to find someone my own age apparently. Huh, maybe I just might then. See what he thinks about that.

My fingers itch to reach for my phone and ask for Scott's number. See what his apology is made of. *Don't do it, Sarah.* My mind screams at me. Sighing, I reach for the TV remote instead and watch *Celebrity First Dates.* I take some comfort in there being people out there as useless at love as I am.

Other than checking in on the twins a couple of times, I continue watching trashy television shows until the clock ticks around closer to eleven. Then I decide to go up to my own room. I don't want to see Emmett when he gets home. He'll have probably had a drink and I couldn't handle it if he spoke about me being a kid anymore, or if he went the other way and alcohol made him make a move.

If there ever was to be something between us, and I know that's not happening, but if there was, Emmett needs to come to me sober and committed.

The babies look so peaceful fast asleep. The light from the hallway illuminates the room just enough for me to look at them. I'm already getting attached and it's only been a week. Closing the door behind me softly as to not disturb them, I head into my room. I have a monitor in there which I switch on as tonight's my night to see to them if they disturb. Then pyjamas on, I climb into my new bed. It's a double and its mattress is so comfortable, a memory foam that moulds to my body. The plump duvet feels like I'm in a cloud and I pull it right up to my chin letting my head sink into my new pillow.

This isn't so bad, Sarah, is it? I think, my toes curling as I stretch and enjoy my new room.

My mind starts to remember another bed of the night before, so I change my thoughts onto what I'd like to do tomorrow until sleep claims me.

I HEAR a baby cry and looking at my alarm clock I see it's only 1:18am. I was sure they'd sleep through. Shit. I drag myself out of bed and put on my robe, pulling it tight around me as I walk back to the babies' room, where I find Emmett standing in the doorway.

"I just thought I'd say goodnight, but I tripped over my own foot and woke Elouise up." He looks at me guiltily.

"You been home long?"

"Cab brought me back half an hour ago. Bar did a lock-in."

"Are you going to bed now then? I'll make sure Elouise settles back down."

"I'm not drunk. I'm a bit merry but I'm not drunk. My babies are the most beautiful things ever, aren't they? I'm not just biased."

I smile at him. "They are, though I do think you are also a tiny bit biased, but what parent wouldn't be? Now why don't you go get in bed and get some sleep?"

"What's the rush? Might have a coffee. Do you want one?"

"No. I'm in bed sleeping."

"Oh, did I wake you? Sorry."

"Come on, Emmett, let's get you into bed." He's clearly tired, and a little bit sozzled. I bet my mum is in a similar predicament with my dad. Making sure Elouise is back settled and comfortable, I push Emmett out of the room and into the direction of his own. "Go get undressed and I'll bring you a coffee up if you want one."

"You're an angel, Sarah. I really think you're an angel."

"Okay, there you go." I open his door and indicate for him to walk in.

"Come on, Emmett." He begins to talk to himself. "Gotta sleep on your own tonight, mate."

I feel myself tense. This is why I wanted to

avoid him after he'd had a drink. I didn't want any conversation about the night before.

He turns to me and I pray to God that he doesn't ask me to join him. I needn't have worried.

"I've got a double date on Friday night with your mum and dad. A double date."

My mouth drops open.

Emmett moves and lies down on his bed, kicking his shoes off. I watch for a moment as he gets comfortable, clearly going to sleep on top of the covers fully dressed.

Well, he didn't waste much time. That's the boundaries clearly drawn.

We're dating.

Other people.

THE TWINS SLEPT SOUNDLY through to seven am. They are already responding well to a bedtime bath, a final drink of warmed milk and being placed in their cots in a dimly lit room. I'm going to talk to Emmett later about blackout curtains because they make all the difference in keeping the room dark and babies asleep. I'd set my alarm for six thirty and got a quick shower and managed a few mouthfuls of a hot drink before I heard them stir on the monitor, so I was calling it a win. I changed nappies, got them dressed and fed and took them into the living room to play while gentle snores emanated from Emmett's room.

All I could think about was Emmett going on a date. I wondered if I knew who they'd set him up with. My parents had a few friends who were now divorced. Feeling annoyed and fidgety, I phoned Reese.

"Give me his number."

"Whose?" She said in an innocent voice.

"You know whose."

"Are we not talking about this?"

"We never talk about this."

She rattles off his number and I write it down. I check everyone's okay, but she doesn't stay on long as Breanna starts crying.

While I'm in a determined mood I text Scott.

Sarah: It's Sarah... Fletcher. You want to talk?

I WAIT. Ten minutes later my phone pings. I'm on the floor playing with the babies. Reaching for it on the sofa, I read the reply.

Scott: **Yes. It's been a long time. I want to explain.**

Sarah: **There's really no need.**

Scott: **I think there is. Can you meet me at Tony's Bar at eight? It's just down from InHale.**

Sarah: **I don't know...**

Scott: **Please. Just give me half an**

**hour. Then if you want to leave that's
fine.**

Sarah: Okay. Tony's at eight.

**Scott: Thank you. You won't
regret it.**

BUT AS I put my phone down, I feel like I'm
already regretting it. I'm sure no good can come of
opening myself up to Scott Sullivan again.

EMMETT FINALLY MAKES his way downstairs
just after ten thirty. He walks into the room,
seemingly taking all the air with him. Yawning, he
moves into a stretch which lifts up his black t-shirt
revealing skin I just want to lick.

"Morning, everyone." He whisks Louis up into

his arms and kisses him all over his face. "How's my lil Louis monster this morning?" Louis giggles.

"Sleep well?" I ask.

"Like the dead. Knowing you were here to take care of the babies... it meant I felt I could relax for the first time in a long time."

"It wasn't in any way due to the copious amounts of alcohol in your system then?" I raise a brow.

He smiles. "Do you know. That night out with your dad did me the world of good. Again, because I knew my babies had you." He places Louis down and picks up Elouise, kissing her in the same way he'd done Louis. "I let loose a little."

I keep myself from correcting him to a lot. Bless him. It made me realise he hadn't had much of a life this past year.

"And you have your date to look forward to on Friday night, so there's that." I remind him.

"Oh God." Emmett's face drains of all colour. "I forgot that. Your parents arranged a double date. I need to cancel."

"No." I protest. "You need to go. It will do you good." I jump up. "Now while you're with the twins what would you like for breakfast? Also, afterwards can we sit and do a meal plan and shopping list for the week and then I'll get the food ordered. Oh, and I took note of you saying I don't have to be around all the time on a weekend, so I've arranged to go out tonight."

"Oh." Emmett looks up. "Anywhere nice?"

"Just out for a drink." I say, not feeling like I want to declare who I'm meeting right now. It would just make things awkward. "So I'll get our evening meal done and then I'll get ready and head straight out after that if that's okay?"

"Hey, I'm not your keeper. You go have fun. And I'll get up with the kids in the night so if you want to have a blow out feel free."

I shake my head. "No, I'm not drinking. I prefer to know I'm in complete control of my actions."

"I'm all for that. Wouldn't be going on a double date if I'd not had a couple of extra pints."

"She might be lovely." I counter.

"It's just going to be weird. Out with your mum and dad but not with Louisa. Awkward and weird." His tummy rumbles.

"Looks like I'd better get cooking." I say and I leave the room so there's no more talk of his dead wife and new date.

. . .

WE DO THE SHOPPING LIST, I do a few bits of housework and we once again head off down to the park as it's another fresh day.

"How's the head?"

"Better for coffee, food, and this fresh air. I forgot your dad can drink me under the table."

I smile.

"Sounds like they have their hands full at home with Luke and his family?"

"Yeah. I love my brother dearly, but he needs to grow up. It's about time he and Liv took responsibility for themselves and stopped going from one mistake to another. She's pregnant again. They have no home, and they're overstaying their welcome at my parents."

"They'll find their way. Anyway, it's for your mum and dad to deal with it. I'm dreading my two having problems I have to deal with."

"I think you've awhile yet."

"I just think about the kind of stuff mum's do with daughters. The talks and stuff, you know?"

"Emmett. That's years away and you might have met someone else and settled down by then. Elouise might not have her mum, but she might have someone she can love and talk to."

"You're right. I'm panicking. Come on, my

hands are freezing off. Let's get to the cafe and I'll buy us both a coffee to thaw our hands out."

"Ooh, I hope they have cookies."

Emmett laughs, "You and cookies. I don't know how you stay so slim."

LATER THAT NIGHT after we've eaten and everything is washed and put away, I change into a simple top and jeans, ready to catch a Tube into London centre. The doorbell rings and I think nothing of it until Emmett's voice shouts, "Sarah, it's for you."

As I walk down the stairs, Emmett looks at me strangely, a pulse ticking in his cheek. Then he stands aside revealing Scott. Emmett walks away, the door banging behind him.

"Surprise!" Scott announces. "I popped to my aunties, and so nipped around to yours and asked for your current address. Thought it'd be nicer if I picked you up. We could go get a drink around here somewhere instead?"

"Yeah, okay. Let me just grab my bag." I'd left it on the kitchen counter when we'd come back from the park.

"I'll wait for you in the car."

"Okay."

Walking back through the hallway, I find Emmett pacing in the kitchen. He holds out my bag. "Looking for this?"

"Yes, thank you."

"You didn't say you had a date."

"I didn't know I had to." I bit back. "I'll try not to be too late back."

"Take all the time you need; but remember, don't bring him back here."

Snatching my bag out of his hand, I turn away from him and walk out of the kitchen. Maybe I do need a good drink after all.

16

EMMETT

She's out on a fucking date.

A fucking date.

No wonder she was so keen for me not to cancel mine on Friday night. Clearly what happened between us the other night meant a hell of a lot more to me than it did to her. The thought of spending an evening with another woman fills me with dread.

Things have been so natural and easy between us. When I started talking earlier about having a woman in Elouise's life, all I could picture was Sarah, not that I was going to tell her that. She would be so good with all that kind of stuff, *those* conversations that even though they're years away already fill me with dread.

I insisted that Sarah leave the cleaning up after dinner so she could go and get ready. If I knew who she'd be spending the evening with, I might not have been so kind. She looked beautiful, even if a little windswept from our walk earlier before we headed upstairs to get changed but when she descended the stairs she looked stunning. She hadn't gone to all that much effort—she wasn't dressed up to the nines—but she looked effortlessly gorgeous. I'd have thought she was meeting a friend if I weren't the one to answer the door.

Only a blind man would miss how attractive the young man was who was filling my doorway with his wide, muscular frame. One look at him and it was like a baseball bat to my chest.

He is the kind of man she should be with. He's the one she should be spending her Friday night's with. Not an old git like me.

With the twins already in bed and asleep, I spend the longest time handwashing all the dishes in an attempt to keep myself distracted. It doesn't work and I end up almost scrubbing the pattern from the plates. The plates my dead wife chose with our wedding gift vouchers. A lump the size of a fucking football climbs up my throat. Could my life get any more dramatic?

When I look at the clock on the oven, it's barely been an hour since she walked out of the house.

I check on the twins. Both sleeping soundly.

I check my phone. Zero messages or phone calls.

I rattle around the house, picking up the odd stray toy that's rolled off under the sofa and sort out the junk drawer in the kitchen before I run out of steam. There's only one thing to do when I'm feeling restless like this, but I hate going to my home gym when there's no one in the house with the twins. I know the monitor works out there, but it still makes me worry.

Taking the stairs two at a time, I change into a pair of joggers and a white shirt before grabbing the baby monitor from my bedside table and I make my way out.

I turn the monitor up as loud as it'll go and I ensure the screen's not going to go to sleep and I secure it right in my line of sight.

My heart's already racing when I step up onto the treadmill and my muscles are locked tight.

Focusing on images of Sarah sitting across from that guy, I hit the start button and make quick work of upping the speed until the sweat starts running down my back.

My legs burn, my chest aches, but for the first time since being inside Sarah on Friday night, I feel some kind of normal.

Working out has always been my escape. If work ever got too much or I had a fight with Louisa, or more likely the one who came before her, then I'd always escape to the gym. It wasn't until we moved here that I had enough space to set up my own. It worked out perfectly while the twins were tiny. I would let them sleep in their Moses baskets while I worked out. They loved the steady beat of my feet hitting the belt. They used to sleep so hard I'd get incredible workouts in. Along with their cute faces, it was what helped get me through.

I lose track of the time. The only things I'm aware of are that my babies are safe and sleeping soundly and my own heart is pounding in my chest as I move back and forth on the running machine.

It's not until there's a loud slam behind me that I'm pulled from my little sanctuary and back into the real world.

Looking over my shoulder, Sarah's eyes are wide in panic, her own chest heaving up and down as if she's just run her own marathon.

"Fucking hell, Emmett. I thought something had happened. I thought you'd left the twins—"

"What? I'd never leave them," I say after having slowed to a stop.

"I know. I do *know* that but when I couldn't find you, but they were both asleep upstairs, I just panicked. I've been running around the house like a madwoman trying to figure out where you might be hiding.

"Well, you found me." I know she's on the verge of hysterics but knowing she spent the night staring at another man, doing God knows what, I'm not really in the mood to soothe her.

Standing, I reach for my t-shirt that I discarded some time ago and use it to wipe my sweaty face.

Her eyes follow my movements, her heart clearly still racing from her earlier panic, but when her gaze drops to my chest, I can't help but wonder if it's suddenly for an entirely different reason.

She's wearing the same jeans and t-shirt she was when she went out and it doesn't look like it's been crumpled at all. The thought has heat surging through my body.

"Did you have a good night?" My voice comes out hoarse even to my own ears.

"It was good, thank you."

"Was he a gentleman?"

Her eyes harden as her lips press into a thin line. "I think it's best if I keep my personal life just that. Personal."

"You're probably right. But it doesn't stop me wondering if you're still in need of a kiss goodnight."

I take a step closer and she just as quickly takes one back. There's a warning in her eyes, one that I should damn well take on board, but thoughts of her sitting with him all night have driven me almost to insanity. I need to know if he touched her. And more so, I need to know if she allowed it. If she could so easily cast aside what happened between us and focus on someone else because I know damn well that I've not been able to.

Every time I close my eyes, all I can see is her writhing beneath me. Her perfectly pink nipples, hard and begging for me to wrap my lips around them. All I can think about is how tight she was when I slid inside of her, how her pussy rippled with pleasure when I was fully seated.

I take another step followed swiftly by another. She rushes to back away but she's at a disadvantage because she soon bumps into the wall.

Her palms flatten against it as her eyes fly

around the small space, trying to find an escape. But that's not going to happen yet. Not until I've found the answers I need to stop me going crazy.

I stop when there's only a slither of space between our bodies. Her sweet floral scent fills my nose and my mouth waters for a reminder of just how fucking good she tastes.

"You didn't answer my question." The second my lips move, her eyes drop to them. The action tells me everything I need to know, but I'm not letting her off that easily.

"You didn't ask one."

I rack my brain for the words I did say to her and realise that she's right.

"Silly me." I tilt my head to the side and run my eyes over every single one of her features before dropping down to her breasts. I can see her nipples puckering behind the fabric and fuck if it doesn't make me hard as fucking nails. If she were to look down, there'd be no denying what I want right now. My joggers don't do a great job of hiding what's down there on the best of days, let alone when I'm this fucking desperate.

Looking up at her from under my lashes, her breath catches and I lean in towards her ear. "Did he kiss you goodnight, Sarah?"

My hand lifts until my fingers wrap around her ribs. She gasps, her body jolting from the sensation I also feel shooting up my arm. My thumb brushes the underside of her breast and she obviously trembles. She needs this just as badly as I do.

"Sarah?"

Moan.

"Answer me. Did. He. Kiss. You?"

Her head moves just a fraction and I breathe a sigh of relief but not fully, not until I hear her say the words. "N- No. He... He didn't k- kiss me."

"Good." My hand slips higher until my palm is full of her soft breast and I slam my lips to hers.

Her entire body tenses and her hands press against my bare chest. For a moment I think she's going to push me away, but then she sags back against the wall, her hand climbing up until she wraps it around the back of my neck and pulls me against her.

My hard planes fit perfectly against her soft curves. A needy moan falls from her lips as I slip my hand up the smooth skin of her stomach in search of her breasts. In one quick move I have the cup of her bra down and I'm pinching her nipple, desperate to hear the little moans of pleasure she makes when I do so. I lap them up like a junkie getting his next hit.

Grinding my hips against her, I try to find some kind of friction to stem the red-hot need racing through my veins to take her right this second.

Reluctantly, I release her breasts and move back down to her waistband. I need her, I need to feel her coming apart beneath me.

My fingers slip into her jeans and then her knickers. I'm millimetres away from finding out just how wet she is for me, how badly she needs me when the one and only noise that could end this rings out in the silent space around us.

A baby's cry.

"Fuuuuck," I roar, slamming my hand down against the wood at the side of her head. Her eyes widen in horror, her body locked up tight in fear.

My chest heaves as I lift my hand to my hair and turn away from her. I was so close to getting what I needed but they stopped me. They stopped me doing exactly what I shouldn't have been. At least someone has the power to because it seems I'm too weak. I'm too weak to stay away from the one woman I never should have touched in the first place.

When I look back over my shoulder, she's gone.

Not a second later does the door to the shed slam shut and I see her retreating back as she runs up the garden path.

"Fuck," I roar, even louder than the first time before my fist connects with the rough wall in front of me.

17

SARAH

What the hell was I thinking, letting him touch me like that? Thank goodness for the baby crying. I enter the twins' room only to find it was one of those cries they make in their sleep. Now there's not a peep from them. At least it means I can go to my room now. The last thing I need is Emmett making his way up here, complicating things, making me want things I can't have.

Tonight had been confusing enough, making me rethink the past as I'd believed it happened...

I get into Scott's car.
"You look lovely, Sarah. Though I always thought you did. Adulthood looks good on you though."

"Thanks." I don't reciprocate. From what I'd heard, he didn't need any compliments, his ego was massive anyway.

"So any requests for where we go?"

I shrug my shoulders. "Wherever you like. I'm not in any rush to get back."

It was funny because I'd decided earlier that I'd have a quick drink with Scott, give him an hour maximum to talk and then I'd rush back to my room, the twins, and the thing I didn't seem to want to admit to myself, Emmett. However after his little alpha male demonstration, I was happy to stay out late now, even if it was with Scott.

"Okay, I know a good pub with a great view. Though if I'm looking at you, any pub will have a great view."

I sigh. "Scott. Don't start with your patter. I've heard all about it and while I hear it gets lots of women into your bed, I've been there, done that. We're out to talk about the past and clear the air. Nothing more, okay? Otherwise, drop me off at the pub and then fuck off."

He turns to me, a smirk on his lips. "What bit your arse? Was it that guy who side-eyed me at the door?"

"Nope."

"If you say so. But he looked like he wanted to snap my neck on the doorstep."

"That's my boss, Scott."

"Wouldn't stop me."

"I don't think a dog van would be able to capture you and your stud behaviour."

"Have you been talking to Suki? She calls me a mutt."

"Ohhhh, is this the woman who doesn't like you? Reese told me I had something in common with a woman you worked with. I can't wait to find out more."

"She's a twat."

I like her already.

We walk into the bar and Scott really has chosen a nice place. It's all warm tones and the seats at the back overlook a stream. There are a few log fires giving out heat and a warming glow.

"Where do you want to sit?" Scott asks me.

"Window seat okay?" I know it's probably a bit chillier over there, but that view is amazing.

"This is where I would normally say wherever you sit near me the view is amazing, but I won't because you've told me not to."

I sigh and shake my head. "Go and get me a glass of white wine."

While he's at the bar, I take time to look at him. He's about six feet one now, with dark brown hair that looks black. It's cut shorter on the sides and is styled on top with paste I guess. Thick dark eyebrows frame his almost coal-coloured eyes, and eyelashes that a woman would kill for make him far too beguiling. I know why I fell for him. He can make himself look charming, vulnerable, and tempting. He's a chameleon. I fell for that years ago. I won't be falling for it again. He's flirting now, running a hand through his hair and looking bashful as the female bartender pours what looks like a Coke. I know at the precise point he orders my wine as her face sets and her eyes traverse the bar until they land on me and narrow. Little does she know she's welcome to him. My own mind is full of a certain boss of mine, despite my inner pleas for it to stop.

I carry on my appraisal of Scott while watching him walk back over. The black long sleeve t-shirt he's wearing is a tight fit to show off the toned physique underneath. His blue skinny jeans hug his thighs, his calves, his arse, and show he's not lacking in the packing department. Though I know that anyway.

Time and other partners showed me that there's no wonder my first time really hurt.

Scott places my wine on the table.

"Thanks." I pick it up and take a sip. The fruity flavours and the coldness excite my taste buds. I smack my lips. "That's a good one."

"Good thing about coming out with someone who works in a restaurant. I know my food and wine."

There's a cool draft coming from the window, but I welcome it in keeping me alert. In not falling for his charm.

"So how long have you worked at InHale?" I stare out at the light dancing off the moving water.

"Five years now. First thing I've committed to, to be honest." My head snaps to his.

"Yep, I'm actually admitting things about myself to you. But it's for one night only. Don't tell anyone. Tomorrow I'm back to Scott the sexy seducer."

"I'd better make the most of it then. So tell me why you took my virginity, disappeared, and never contacted me again."

I'm not expecting what leaves his mouth.

"Because I was in a psychiatric unit."

My mouth drops open. "What?"

He takes a deep inhale. "My mum had been really poorly. Breast cancer. I was seventeen. My dad had walked out on us when I was a year old. My mum was all I had. Her illness had started when I was fifteen myself and so I'd been caring for her when it was time to study for my exams. The pressure was becoming too much, but I carried on. My mum could see I was struggling, and we did our best between us but what could she do? She needed me. As much as she didn't want to rely on me, when she was puking her guts up, she had no choice."

I can tell from Scott's expression that his mind is back there reliving everything.

"When mum started to get better she sent me to my auntie and uncles house saying I needed a break. I didn't want to go but she insisted, saying I was to enjoy some time as a teenager, to make some friends and give her some time to herself to rediscover who she was as she finished treatment and began to recover. Anyway, I went to my aunties and I did what my mum had asked. I made a ton of friends, including you. Then I found a new interest... sleeping with girls. I was a horny teenage boy. Thought with my dick, not my brain."

I rolled my eyes.

"I'm sorry but that's how it was. I liked you, Sarah.

You were a lovely girl. But I was a horny teenager. Girls are so much more invested in everything. The night of your birthday when you saw me drinking in the woods, I'd had a call from my mother. She was ready for me to come home, but she had some news for me. Unbeknown to me, while she was ill, my dad had heard about it and had gotten in touch. They were back together. I couldn't believe it. We'd not heard a word from him, as far as I knew.

"Turns out he'd not been so far away. A couple of towns over with another wife. A family he left to come back to ours. I'm not proud but I lost myself in you that next day and night, took comfort from your craving for me. You wanted me so desperately. I didn't tell you I had to go home."

There's no light in Scott's face as he continues. "I got home and nothing was as I'd known it. It was like my mother had died because the one that was living in my house wasn't the mother I'd left. My father brought no end of drama with the fact he'd left another relationship and after one particular incident where he took me out to meet my half-brother, my mind fractured. I ended up in hospital for a few months."

"I had no idea, obviously." I say. "When you sent me that text, saying you'd enjoyed spending time

with me, but you weren't keeping in touch, I was devastated, and then you blocked me."

He shook his head. "I didn't have my phone. I never even sent you the text. One of my parents would have sent it."

"What happened after that?"

Scott rises from his seat. "Oh we don't need to get into the life of Scott Sullivan. Let me get you another glass of wine and catch up with your life, shall we?"

And with that he doesn't say another word of the past.

Scott is good company, but as the evening wears on, the cocky Scott I had the company of at the beginning returns to the fore. It's only when he pulls up outside Emmett's and double checks that I won't tell anyone what he confessed that the real Scott buried somewhere deep inside appears again.

"I won't say a word. I'm just glad we got to clear up what happened. It affected me for years but now I totally get it. You had your issues, but even so, I was a teenage girl with a broken heart and you were a randy teen." I smile.

"Sorry."

"Nothing to be sorry for as it turns out."

"Would you like to go out again sometime?" Scott
asks, quickly adding, "as friends, I mean. I don't
want a relationship, ever, but I could use a friend."
"Sure." I nod. "I'd like that."
"And feel free to use me to make that guy in there
jealous." He grins as I depart the car.
I don't reply, because to do so would be
acknowledging something I'm trying to deny.

BUT AS I climb into bed and I think about what just happened between myself and Emmett, I can't deny how I feel any more. Whether we should be doing this or not, my body craves his touch.

Slipping down under the duvet I picture the scene from the gym; Emmett's desperate, animalistic gaze. His hand on my breast, pinching my nipple. I move my hand to my breast under my pyjama top and replay his moves, then move my hand lower, dipping down beyond the waistband of my bottoms and dipping a finger through my wetness teasing at my clit. My fantasy takes what happened and imagines what would have come next. My fingers become Emmett's in my imagination, dipping within me and teasing at my bud. Then it's just not enough and I sit up and reach into my bedside cabinet, rustling through my underwear drawer until I find the dildo I have hidden at the bottom.

A quiet knock at my door has me freeze. I don't make another sound until I hear footsteps walk away.

But I'm too far gone with lust to stop and imagining the dildo is Emmett's dick I thrust it inside me, moving it in and out as I moan, crying out his name as I come hard.

18

EMMETT

Lifting my forearm to the wall of the shed, I place my forehead against it as I try to get my breathing under control.

That shouldn't have happened. I know it shouldn't. She knows it shouldn't, but it's like I'm powerless to resist. I've had a taste of her now and my craving for more is only getting worse as time goes on.

It's just because she's the first after so long, I try to tell myself. I'm sure I'd feel the same of any woman who put an end to my never-ending dry spell.

As much as I try to believe myself, I know it's not true. Sarah's not just a body that I'm craving.

How I'm feeling for her runs deeper than that and it's scary as fuck.

She should be here helping me get my life on track so I can go back to work. She isn't meant to be bringing me back to life in ways I hadn't really realised had died.

Sucking in a deep breath, I turn everything off and head back up to the house.

Although all the lights are still on, it's in silence. I guess whatever was up with the twins is sorted. Either that or she's up there soothing one of my babies.

The image of her with them cuddled into her arms pops in my head and it makes my heart ache.

I've longed to see them in their mother's arms. I always will. They'll never get to experience what a wonderful person she was and equally, she'll never know what amazing children we made together. But seeing them being cared for with a woman's touch that isn't my mothers, well it still hits me hard. It's what they've needed. I'm sure Sarah's magic tricks at bedtime do help but I'm sure it's more her presence that helps them sleep at night. Her soft and caring way with them. She's just a natural.

That thought has me stopping in my tracks and

a shiver runs down my spine. I've not forgotten how old Sarah is—or isn't—but the reality that she should be meeting someone her own age so that she can settle down and have children of her own is a sobering thought.

This thing between us has to end. I have to be the grown up that I am, the responsible father that I am and allow her to live the life she deserves.

With my shoulders dropped in defeat, I head up the stairs. I intend on going straight to the bathroom for a shower and then to lock myself in my room, but the second I step onto the landing my body freezes.

A soft moan fills the air around me. Taking a quiet step forward, I hear it again and realise it's coming from Sarah's room.

I close the space, originally wanting to make sure that she's okay. I realise that she could be angry or upset after what happened between us and I should probably check that she's okay and apologise.

I knock lightly, intending to do just that but not a second after do I hear my own name. She's... fuck...

My cock immediately stands to attention as realisation as to what's going on just the other side of the door hits me. My name is followed up with another moan of pleasure and my hand trembles as it lifts to the door handle.

Every muscle in my body aches to step inside and see if the image I have in my head of her laid out on her bed with her fingers between her legs is what's really happening. My mind runs away with me as I picture climbing up the bed and immediately licking up her juices from her recent orgasm.

Fuck.

My fingers close around the handle with an almost painful grip. An internal debate going on inside my head. My cock wants me to walk in and take what's mine. I mean, she called my name so there's no doubt in my mind who she was imagining just a few seconds ago. But my head... my head still knows that I should be doing the right thing.

It's long seconds before I force my legs to move and take a giant step back.

Closing the bathroom door, I flick the lock in the hope it might keep me inside and I fall back against the heavy wood.

My chest heaves, my heart races and my cock throbs.

I desperately try to will the images away that are filling my mind. I know exactly how'd she'd look with her feet on the mattress with her knees spread.

"Fuck." My hands fly to my hair and pull. I can only hope the sharp sting of pain helps to sort my head out. Walking into her room is wrong. It's the wrong thing to do.

Pushing away from the wall, I turn the shower on hot, strip out of my clothes and step under the scalding water. It's punishment for my impure thoughts about the woman in my guest room who is not only my employee, but too young for me and the daughter of my best friend.

My skin prickles under the heat but at no point do I turn it down. Instead, I wrap my fist around my hard cock and tug viciously until I relieve just a little of the frustration that's holding my body hostage.

It does little to help. There's only one thing that could possibly help right now but I won't allow it. I can't. I was weak once, I can't risk it happening again.

I force myself to keep my eyes on the carpet as I let myself out of the bathroom and head straight for my bedroom.

I lie in bed for hours, tossing and turning, trying to clear my head. Every little squeak and creak of the house and my cock lurches thinking that she's coming to find me.

As the hours creep by, the twins still sleeping soundly, I try to figure out what the hell I'm going to say to her in the morning.

Did she know I was there? Did she hear me knock? Did she want me to walk in? Is she now laid there just as frustrated as I am wondering if I'm going to man up?

I drive myself crazy and by the time I hear movement in the twins' room, I'm bursting at the seams with nervous energy.

I get them both ready as quietly as I can, hoping to put off having to see her but I know I'm on borrowed time. She's going to have to come out of her room eventually.

It's not long after we make it downstairs that I hear water running above my head.

My heart begins to race and my stomach turns over knowing that I'll have to look at her soon.

Each thud of her feet on the stairs is like a gunshot through my heart. The anticipation too much to bear.

When she eventually does round the corner

and finds us sitting at the dining table covered in porridge I don't look up. I can't.

She's going to be too beautiful. Too tempting. I make a snap decision, hoping that my indifference will help put a wall up between us.

"So I've decided to go into work today. I'd like to be there for eight." I don't give her the chance to respond. Dropping the bowl and spoon onto the table, I march from the room and up the stairs, leaving her to finish the job I started.

I had no such intention but when I get to my room, I realise that I'm going to have to follow through. The last thing I need is Ross getting suspicious if she were to say something.

Opening my wardrobe, I pull out my old work clothes, ones that haven't even been touched in a year. If I knew this was happening, I'd have put them all through the wash to freshen them up but there's not a lot of time now.

I dress, run some wax through my hair and head back down.

The three of them are now in the living room playing. I drop down onto my haunches and give each twin a kiss goodbye.

"I'll be back for dinner," I say coldly, without so much as looking in her direction and I storm from the house, the door slamming a little too loudly behind me.

THE NEXT FEW days carries on much the same. I avoid being in the same room with Sarah at all costs. If I'm home I tell her that I'll look after the twins so she can get on with other stuff and if she's busy, I ensure I'm as far away from her as possible.

Every night after the twins have gone down, I head to my gym. I'd not really been using it so I guess one good thing could come out of all this.

My impending double date doesn't help my mental state. I don't want to go on any date, let alone a double date with Sarah's parents. The whole situation is laughable. Her dad's trying to set me up and help me move on, yet the only woman I can think about is his daughter, and not just because she's looking after my kids.

My imagination about what she was doing to herself the other night has only gotten wilder. It's one of the reasons I can't look her in the eye because I know it's all I'll be able to see.

I'm just about to head upstairs once she's got the twins settled on Thursday night to change into my gym clothes when Sarah clears her throat.

"If it's okay with you, I'm going to go out."

"Of course you can go out. You're not my slave," I bark, so harshly that I reel back a little.

"Oh... I... I just wanted to check you didn't have plans."

"I don't. I'm a single dad to twins, what kind of plans might I have?" I risk a glance at her and immediately hate myself. All the colour's drained from her face and her eyes are full of tears.

My teeth grind with my need to apologise, but before I get a chance, she grabs her bag and runs past me out of the front door.

Well fuck. It really looks like I'm screwing all of this up.

I forgo the trip to my home gym in favour of a glass of whiskey and the sofa. I stare at some police documentary on the TV, but I have no clue what it's really about. I'm too lost in my own head.

I've no clue where she's gone, she could be out with anyone, but of course I assume it's the guy from the other night taking her out on another date.

I should be happy for her. He looked like a decent guy, plus he was young enough for her. It's what I should want for her. But I don't. I don't even want to imagine her looking at him like she did me the night we threw caution to the wind while celebrating her freedom. The thought of him touching her like I did lights a fire in my belly. One that tells me that I can't be down here when she gets back.

It's just before ten when I make my way upstairs and only twenty minutes later when I hear her come in. She potters around for a bit before shutting herself inside her room.

It's for the best. Let her hate you. Let her find what she really needs, are the words on repeat in my mind as I urge sleep to claim me.

MY NEED TO stay away from Sarah has meant that I've basically returned to work early. I spend almost all day Friday in Ross' office either in meetings about clients that I'm going to take over on or just generally catching up with work policies and procedures that have changed in my time away. At no point though does he allow me to forget about tonight. If he's told me once that Celia is beautiful and sexy then he's told me a million times.

"Our table's booked for eight. Do not be late

and do not bail on us," Ross warns after I've packed up ready to leave for the day.

"I'll be there." The fact he's worried about me being a no show proves just how miserable I am about the whole thing.

"This is going to be really good for you, Emmett. You can get a little of your life back, have some fun." His eyebrows wiggle at the suggestion and I want the ground to swallow me up knowing that I've had some fun recently and it was with the one woman he wouldn't want me anywhere near, well... besides his wife, I'm sure.

The restaurant he's booked, InHale, is the one Sarah suggested as a possible for my fortieth birthday. It's the must-visit restaurant of the moment according to Ross. I know it's going to be flashy, but that doesn't stop my eyes widening slightly when my Uber pulls up out the front. Clearly Ross really wants to impress tonight.

I find the three of them waiting for me in the entrance and I'm immediately introduced to Celia, who is really very beautiful and sexy, although she doesn't affect me in any way. Anyone with eyes could appreciate that she's a good-looking woman. What really catches my attention though is the waiter. He's familiar and it's not until he comes over to take our order and his eyes widen in recognition that I realise who he is. He's the arsehole who's been taking Sarah out. My hackles instantly rise, my fingers tightening on my glass of water in an attempt to keep things civil.

If he's shocked to see me then he doesn't show it, but he knows full well who I am, and he makes sure I know it with a little wink as he walks away to get our drinks.

"Sarah mentioned coming here to a party, so we thought we'd check the place out. Luckily, they'd had a cancellation because the place is usually booked solid." Ross said.

"Wow, the waiter is a dish. No wonder this place is always so busy," Sarah mum, Marie says much to Ross' horror.

My date for the evening agrees, her eyes following him over to the bar, but I couldn't give a shit. I knew before I even turned up that I wouldn't be interested in anything she had to offer.

I keep my eye on the waiter all night, to the point that the others have to keep making a point to drag me back into the conversation. I'm too desperate to find out if he's any good for Sarah or not. I quickly come to the conclusion that he's not, based on the fact he flirts with anything with a heartbeat.

Infuriatingly, Scott works out who Ross and Marie are and comes over to the table to introduce himself.

"Are you Ross and Marie Fletcher?"

"We are," Marie says, looking intrigued.

"I'm Scott Sullivan; you live next door to my auntie."

Realisation dawns on Marie's face. "Goodness me, what happened to that young boy? I'll have to tell our Sarah I saw you."

"I actually caught up with her. She came to her friend's engagement party here. We've been out for a drink. Wonderful daughter you have." His gaze drifts over me again, a smirk to his lip.

"Oh that's fantastic."

They spend another few minutes catching up and then Scott has to go deal with another table. I'm glad because I felt another five minutes and I may have punched him in the jaw. Marie starts saying how she wonders if Scott and Sarah might get together and I'm glad when Ross asks for the bill.

. . .

BY THE TIME the bill has been paid and we stand to leave, I've most definitely had enough. Celia smiles at me and places her arm on mine but I don't really give her the time of day other than to thank her for a wonderful evening. It's totally insincere and I'm sure no one misses it.

Ross eyes me curiously as he urges Celia forward to give us a little privacy, not that we need it.

"I'll see you Monday, yeah?" I call to him, putting an end to this torture and the second my Uber pulls out outside the restaurant I'm gone.

19

SARAH

He's out on a date. With my mum and dad and some woman his own age. Well he couldn't have made it any clearer this past week if he tried that he's not interested in me romantically. I hate it. I can admit that to myself, but I do understand. The twins have to be the most important thing here and so regardless of the attraction between us, we just have to move past it.

He's been like a bear with a sore head all week. It's been awkward but I'm sticking with it all for now because I'm sure at some point soon we'll be able to get back to a decent working relationship, and also, because I don't want to go back to sofa surfing at my parents' house. Also, I love these little babies, and I want to keep looking after them. I'm attached already and their dad being grumpy isn't anything I can't handle.

He'd looked so attractive tonight when he'd come downstairs. When he'd kissed his babies I think my ovaries actually exploded. And then the door banged and he was gone. I've spent the whole night getting the twins down and then cleaning and tidying in order to keep myself occupied because otherwise my mind goes to the restaurant and him sitting there with his date.

Is she attractive?

Are they hitting it off?

Will he bring her back here?

Is he going to do all the things to her he did to me while I'm here listening to it?

I almost take the varnish off the table I clean it so hard. There's nothing left for me to do eventually but to go to bed, but for some reason I don't want to go. Why should I? I decide I'm going to stay on the sofa until he gets home and then if he has brought a date back with him, I'll even offer to make them a drink before I go to bed. I'll let him think it doesn't affect me at all because that's the best way of dealing with this situation.

Last night I'd gone to Reese's. I needed to get out of the house and to be honest I deliberately left

Emmett under the impression that I had a date. I tried to tell myself it was so he'd feel free to enjoy his own date tonight, but who am I kidding? I did it to punish him, in the hope that he felt the same heavy stone in his stomach that I feel now.

I must fall asleep on the sofa because the next thing I know my eyes flicker open and Emmett is standing in the doorway, the light of the hall illuminating his body. His eyes look hungry, desperate, as they roam over my body. I realise my skirt has ridden up while I'm asleep, revealing my thighs. I quickly pull it down and sit up.

"Did you have a good time?" I mumble sleepily.

"No," he says snappily.

Great, he's still in a mood.

I rub at my eyes. "Do you want a hot drink before I go on up to bed?"

"No, I fucking do not." he snaps.

That wakes me up a little more.

"Look, Emmett. I get what you're trying to do here. Put some space between us. The twins come first. I know that. I'm doing the same. But do you have to be such a twat to me? Can't you be civil? It's making things really hard."

He stalks into the room. There's no other word

for the slow way he moves closer. He takes the chair opposite the sofa.

"I've spent the evening sat talking to your parents. Looking your father in the eye as he asks me if I'm pleased with your work, while in my head I'm undressing you, stripping off your clothing and feasting on your cunt.

"Meanwhile Ross is trying desperately to get me to communicate with the woman he'd set me up with. She's attractive, she's my age, and when I did pay her the smallest bit of attention she seemed nice. But instead I found my attention was taken up with the waiter. The same waiter who took you out the other night." He looks feral right now, his mouth curled in a sneer.

"You went to InHale?"

"Yes, because you'd told them how nice it was. So I spent the evening wondering if you'd let him inside you. Hoping for your sake that you hadn't because he spent the whole evening flirting with other women and accepting phone numbers, and hoping for my sake that you hadn't because although I'm trying desperately to tell myself no over and over again, the only person who should be inside you is me."

I gasp at his words. He leaves his seat and

kneels at the side of me on the sofa. "I'm probably going to regret this tomorrow, but tonight I simply don't fucking care, Sarah."

His eyes laser me with their intense stare.

"Did you fuck him?"

I shake my head. "No."

"Good."

He pushes my skirt back up my thighs and I don't even attempt to stop him because I want him just as much as he wants me. And if tomorrow the same thing happens and we don't talk about it again, then so be it. Tonight, I'll take all he can give me so I have something to remember if it never gets repeated.

I lift my hips to assist as Emmett pulls my panties down my thighs and off. He pulls me to the edge of the sofa and then pushes my thighs apart, his eyes feasting on my centre. His gaze is hungry. His mouth descends and fastens on me, and I moan as his warm tongue sweeps across my clit. He breaks off and looks back up at me.

"I heard you the other night, Sarah. Did you get off thinking about me and calling my name?"

"Yes." I admit.

"I want to hear you call my name again," he demands as his mouth returns to my core.

His tongue flicks over my clit over and over, then he's pushing two fingers inside me and I ride him hard, my chest heaving, my nipples pebbled under my blouse. We're fully dressed except for my naked bottom half. I look wanton, split apart on the sofa, my skirt pushed up while this man feasts on my pussy. The thought of what we'd look like to someone walking in on us is enough to push me over the edge and I pull his head towards me as I ride his mouth as I tremble against him.

"Emmett." I cry out. "Oh fuck, Emmett."

He swallows the last of my orgasm, licking up my juices and then he quickly sheds his own clothes and strips me out of the rest of mine. He pulls me to my knees so I'm resting over the sofa and his dick edges against my entrance. He guides himself inside me and I sigh at the feeling of fullness. Then he winds my hair around his fist and drags my head up until he can kiss and nibble at my neck. It's so fucking alpha that I can feel my juices running over his cock. He starts to thrust in and out of me. It's hard and rough and I realise he's staking his claim right now. Owning my body. Seeing Scott has brought out his inner caveman.

"Harder," I demand, not able to get enough of

this man. He answers my desires, his hips rocking against me with such force I'm lifted off my knees.

I rock back against him just as hard and we're coated in sweat as we demand satisfaction from the other.

As I feel his balls tighten, I come, pulsing around his cock. Emmett pulls out spraying my back in his cum.

I collapse over the sofa, my breath coming in heavy pants. Emmett moves and I realise he's picked up his shirt as he wipes my back.

Then he scoops me up in his arms and he carries me up to his bedroom where I finally fall asleep after more orgasms than I can count.

OF COURSE, daylight brings with it uncertainty. My eyes open and I wonder as I find myself laid in Emmett's bed, if we're back to employer and employee and if I need to get out of this bed before Emmett wakes up. Carefully, I begin to edge out of his arms.

"No." A voice says firmly.

I turn to him. "N- no?"

"I can't do this anymore, Sarah. Pretending I'm not attracted to you. I know I shouldn't be doing this and I know it's risky, but I want you in my bed."

I'm rendered speechless.

"Oh God. I've fucked things up, haven't I? You don't want that. You want the job. I'm sorry, Sarah. It's difficult, but pretend I never said anything."

I lean forward and answer him with a kiss. My hand moving to grasp his morning wood.

"Shut up, Emmett."

I move over him, sitting across his thighs and impaling myself on his cock. I'm slightly sore from the fucking marathon we enjoyed last night, but the burn feels good as I sink on top of him.

His hands roam over my body, caressing my breasts, and then holding my arse as I lift up and down on him.

I'm moaning in pleasure as I swing my hips.

"God, yes," he moans. "Just like that." He rocks his hips up and pulls me down harder, until once again we're frenzied as we seek our completion. When I feel he's near I get off him, delaying his gratification. Pulling him down the bed, I lower myself over his mouth and ride his face until I'm exploding over him. Then I move and take him in my mouth and suck on him until his own pleasure is spent.

Eventually, the time comes where I need to take a shower. Emmett reluctantly lets me slide out of his arms.

"I'll get the twins up and give them their breakfast and then I'll get my own shower."

"While you shower, I'll get the coffee on and make us a cooked breakfast. I feel like we've worked up an appetite." I smile at him.

"We sure did."

I ENJOY MY SHOWER, feeling the burn between my thighs and smiling. I don't know what's happening next with me and Emmett, but I can't help hoping it's the start of something good.

As I'm fixing breakfast, he's standing behind me kissing my neck.

"I think we're going to have to sit and talk about this, Emmett, because you're putting me off my work."

He nuzzles my neck. "Can we talk about it tomorrow and just enjoy today?"

I turn towards him, "We definitely talk tomorrow."

"Okay," he says taking my lips in his. As I burn the bacon, I fix my hands on my hips.

"See, look what you made me do."

"I'm not hungry for bacon anyway." He pulls my hips towards him and grinds against me. "I'm hungry for you."

I eventually manage to get myself and the twins ready for a trip to the park. Emmett says it gives him an ideal opportunity to deal with some emails. I have the front door open and the twins ready to depart when I realise I forgot my phone. I head into the kitchen to get it while Emmett stands in the doorway watching the twins.

As I brush past him to get back to the doorway he groans and grabbing me pushes my back against the wall.

"Fuck, I can't get enough of you," he says, taking my mouth in his. He's grinding against me and we're kissing, lost in the moment and then suddenly he's not there anymore.

My eyes widen in shock as I realise that while we were lost in the moment my father has walked past the twins and has dragged Emmett away by his shirt.

"Dad," I scream, but I can do nothing but watch as my father pulls back his arm, fist clenched and punches Emmett straight in the gut.

20

EMMETT

One second I've got my lips on Sarah's, claiming her in the way I know I shouldn't be and the next I'm curled up in a fall on my hallway floor writhing in pain.

What the hell?

Coming back to myself, I stare up at a pair of angry eyes that I wasn't expecting and the sound of Sarah screaming as she comes racing to my side.

"Oh my god, Emmett. Are you okay?"

"Get the hell away from him," Ross barks. His stare still not leaving mine. "Let him get up and take it like a man."

"What? No. There will be no fighting. You're friends."

"Exactly. Just one of the many reasons why he

shouldn't have just been... Ugh, I can't even say it. Get your stuff, Sarah. We're leaving."

The pain in my belly subsides enough for me to attempt to stand, well either that or it's the fear of her leaving that has me on my feet.

"No."

"I'm sorry, but you don't get a say in this. You've already taken advantage of this situation. We should have you done for harassment or something."

"You think... Jesus, Ross. I've not done anything wrong here."

"You've prayed on a young girl. Well, that young girl just so happens to be my baby girl and I won't stand for it."

"Dad, no," Sarah wails, getting between the two of us when Ross flexes his fists again. "That's not what this is."

"I told you to go and get your stuff. Why are you still down here?" Ross barks, making Sarah rear back.

"I'm not leaving. This is where I live now. This is where I work."

"I'm not leaving you under his roof any longer. Anything could happen." He must be able to see the guilt on our faces because he roars and lunges forward despite Sarah being in the way. His trembling hand wraps around my neck, but I don't do anything to move it. He has every right to be angry, and I deserve this for touching something that wasn't mine to have. For even believing for a second that we could be something. It was stupid. It was fantasy.

Sarah claws at her dad's arm, but his grip still doesn't let up. His eyes narrow, pure hatred oozing from them. "I thought she'd be safe here. I thought you of all people would treat her with the respect she deserves."

"I- I..." I try to respond but his fingers tighten.

"He has, Dad. He hasn't taken advantage of me. I wanted this just as—"

"ENOUGH." Ross' breathing is heavy, his chest heaving as he tries to contain his anger. "So what are you telling me? You love her, do you?"

My eyes widen in shock. He's clearly serious because he loosens up and allows me to answer.

Opening my mouth to respond, Sarah's inquisitive stare burns into me. She wants the answer to that question too; she needs the reassurance that this is serious, but I don't think I have the words either of them want right now and I refuse to lie to Sarah.

There's something between us. Something big, but it's wrong. We've both said it, we both are aware. So when I manage to form a response it's the one I think she needs. She's twenty-five; she shouldn't be stuck here with an almost forty-year-old with baby twins. She deserves to be out enjoying her youth before she finds the one to do all of this with. The motherfucker from the restaurant maybe. Something explodes inside me at the thought, but I know I need to do right by her.

"N- no. It was just... just a bit of fun."

"No," she sobs and my heart damn near breaks in two but there's only a second before Ross' fist connects with my cheek. "You're lying. That's not what this is." She only just gets the words out as tears drop from her eyes.

Dragging my eyes away, I look to Ross, who's reared back for another shot.

Sarah shouts something else but Ross' punch leaves my ears ringing. I don't miss her running upstairs and then only minutes later returning with a bag and running through the front door, tears streaming down her face.

My body sags against the wall and Ross takes a step back. His eyes run over my face and I wonder if he can see the truth. He knows me better than this. I'd have thought he'd have given me the benefit of the doubt, but his final words prove otherwise.

"Consider yourself lucky if you still have a job come Monday morning."

The slamming of the front door echoes through the house and wakes the twins who'd drifted off to sleep in their buggy.

They both scream, forcing me to put aside everything that just happened in favour of sorting them out.

I have the intention of getting them back out of the buggy and letting them play while I try to wrap my head around what the fuck just happened, but they both scream and wrap their little fists around the straps wanting to go out on the walk that was promised to them.

Caving to their sad little faces, and with my stomach and face aching, I begin pushing them down the street. It's fucking freezing, the wind pierces through my thin t-shirt and whips across my face making it sting even more.

Thankfully, the almost sub-zero temperature means I don't bump into anyone else. I can only imagine what I look like right now.

Eventually, the cold gets too much and I'm

forced to head back before they've fallen back to sleep. It's a sign that I'm going to be in for some fun when I get back but even knowing that, I'm not prepared for the tantrums that follow me closing the front door and turning the heating up.

They throw their toys back at me when I pass them over for them to play with, they scream when I put the TV on in an attempt to distract them, and they tip over the bowls of fruit I cut up thinking that they're hungry. Nothing helps but I know the issue because I'm feeling it too.

I fall down onto the sofa, both the twins still whining on the floor. My head falls back against the cushion and I look towards the front door, at the last place I saw her before she walked out of our lives and left us in this mess.

Lifting my hand, I touch it to my sore and still bleeding lip. By the time I got to the bathroom, I didn't need to look to know that my eye was swollen and that the bruise on my cheek was probably purple and angry.

I haven't had a black eye from fighting since I was about fifteen. I blow out a long breath. That was over a girl too.

Lunch is a battle where I end up wearing more of their beans on toast than they manage to get in their mouths. I change my t-shirt twice before giving it up as a bad job and just sit there topless until they've finished. I just don't have it in me to care.

I'm still trying to clean the kitchen when the sound of a key pushing into the lock stops me in my tracks. My heart slams against my chest as I pray to anyone who might listen that she's come back. That she's talked some sense into her dad and come to allow me to apologise for lying about how I feel about her.

Sadly, when my visitor rounds the corner it's not Sarah's soft, regretful face that greets me but the hard and judgemental one of my mother. The second she gets a look at the state of me, her lips twist in distaste.

"I'm not going to like this, am I?" She guesses correctly.

"Probably not. How about I just make you a coffee and find a clean shirt, then we can forget all about it?"

"Hardly, when I've got to look at your face in that state." Elouise screams and my mum goes running. "Have you upset them as well?" she calls after her, making me groan in frustration. Why does she just assume that whatever's happened is my fault? *Because it is.*

MUM MANAGES to work some magic and not twenty minutes later both twins are in bed and fast asleep. They must have been pretty exhausted after all the crying.

I sip at my coffee, trying to ignore the weight of her stare that makes me feel like a child.

"Go on then. I'm waiting."

I blow out a breath wondering how I explain sleeping with my nanny and then all but falling in love with her in the process.

"I... uh... took something that wasn't mine." I cringe at my words.

"You're going to need to do better than that, son."

"Fine. I'm in love with Sarah."

"Oh, Emmett."

"Yeah. Ross found out and well..." I wave at my face; it's all the evidence she needs to know how well that went.

"By being in love with her, I assume you mean you're sleeping with her?" My lips curl, just hearing those words falling from my mother's lips. "She's almost a child herself, Emmett."

"She's twenty-five. Hardly a child, Mother."

"Young enough to be impressionable."

"Old enough to know her own mind," I counter.

Our stares hold. She's just as stubborn as I am, so it could go either way for who's going to break first. In the end I can't stand her judgemental assessment of the situation any longer.

"I'm in love with her, but I lied."

"Why?"

"Because she deserves better than me. Than this." I gesture to the huge pile of toddler toys in the corner of the room.

"Have you asked her what she thinks?"

"Well... no. But she walked out so..."

"So what, Emmett? I want to sit here and chastise you for going after someone so young but if you truly do love her then I'm happy for you. You just need to decide what you want to do about it. Sit here sulking or fight for what you want?"

She leaves me to my thoughts not long after. Thankfully, the twins are much happier once they've had a long nap, but what's missing is never far from any of our minds. I catch them both looking for her more than once and it breaks my heart that I've ruined that for them.

WHEN I GO to bed that night; for the first time in a year, I walk into the master bedroom and sit myself down on the edge of her bed. The room smells like her and I immediately feel a little better for it, although it doesn't help me with my decision as to whether I did the right thing or not. I want her, there's no doubting that, but she deserves so much more. More than I have to offer.

When I wake the next morning, I'm surrounded by her and I soon remember that I didn't leave her room. Instead, I climbed under her covers and dreamt she was there with me.

BUT I WAKE WITH AN IDEA. It's entirely dramatic, but I think it's something I need to do. A way to sort this mess out. Because I've realised that I need her in my life. It's time to somehow get her back.

21

SARAH

I climb into my dad's car. I daren't even look at him.

"What the hell were you thinking, Sarah? Have you actually slept with him, or has it just been making out in hallways?" He shakes his head, obviously unable to cope with the visuals. "Never mind."

"We've been getting along really well, and I thought it was going somewhere." I'm trying my best to hold in my tears, but I can feel my body trembling.

"Well you heard what he said to me. You were a bit of fun."

I feel like my dad just slapped me in the face. It

had hurt enough hearing it directly from Emmett. I didn't need to hear it a second time.

"You do know he was out on a date just last night, don't you? With someone more his own age. I don't know how I didn't kill him." My dad's voice rises. "God knows what your mother is going to say."

We pull up at a red traffic light and he turns to me. "You just had that drama with the child who accused you of hitting them. You'd think you'd get on with your job and be as professional as possible having managed to find a new one. And it's my friend, Sarah, and my employee. How the fuck am I supposed to work with him or see him again when he's touched my daughter?"

I don't answer because I know he doesn't want me to. He just wants to rant.

My dad's actually quite a placid man. Unless he's wronged or the family is attacked in some way, then he becomes irate and ranty, but it doesn't usually last long. I just need to endure the car journey and then decide where I'm going next.

I watch as he flexes his fingers of his right hand out. He'll be needing ice on those when we get in.

"He wasn't blackmailing you, was he?" Dad

suddenly looks more alert. "Like saying he'll sack you unless you do, erm, things."

"No!" That's it. I love my dad but I've had enough now. "We were attracted to each other, and we slept together. I'm a grown woman, Dad. Can you stop acting like I'm fourteen instead of twenty-five?"

"He's almost forty."

"So what? What does it matter? There are fourteen years between us, not sixty."

"He's my friend."

I sigh. "I know. I'm sorry, Dad. I didn't mean to ruin your friendship or make your workplace difficult. I just really liked him."

"Emmett should have known better."

"Why? Because he's your age? Do you not make mistakes any more then once you're in your forties, Dad? Because I don't mean to be rude, but you have both your kids back home living with you, so somewhere it looks like you fucked up."

"Didn't I just." He spits out.

I look out of the window, still trying to keep it together, swallowing hard.

"I'm sorry, Sarah. And yes, I still do make mistakes. For instance, I recommended you to Emmett. I certainly messed up there."

"No. If he really did think I was just a bit of fun, then I messed up there. Me, Dad. I'm the employee who slept with their boss. Now can we change the subject a bit, because I don't feel like talking about it anymore." Not until we get home and Mum hears all about it.

The last thing I want to do is go home and have to see my mum's reaction. But at the same time the place I want to be most is at home talking to my mum about it.

"Do you know what I do when I need a bit of peace and quiet, a bit of an escape from the house?" My dad asks.

My mouth downturns. Okay so we're not done talking.

"You go call on Emmett."

"Yeah. And he listens to me tell him about all the crap going on with Luke and Liv, and how I can't get a minute's peace and then he'll laugh and point to where the twins are and we'll have a quick beer. Now where do I go? When I want to escape the chaos that is our house, where do I go?"

"Maybe you shouldn't actually be going anywhere, Dad. Just maybe, you should be standing at Mum's side and helping her deal with stuff. I mean, what is going on at home? How long are

Luke and Liv staying? How's Mum doing about the whole thing? I mean that's your takeaway from this whole situation? Not whether or not your daughter is happy, but that you might lose a friend?"

"You're right. Let's not talk about this any more for now." Dad spits out. "In fact, how about for the last part of the journey we don't talk at all. Maybe it will give you some time to reflect on your actions."

Great. If I didn't feel shit enough about what Emmett just said about me; about losing my job; about having to go back to my parents' house again for a short while; I now have to deal with the guilt of ruining my dad's friendship and causing him problems at work.

I feel like my brain is about to explode.

As the remainder of the car ride progresses, my thoughts are all on Emmett. About how he commanded me last night when he came home. How he crowded me in that hallway, and then how he told my father it was just fun.

Life lately seems to keep wanting to punish me, and I don't even have a room I can go and break down in.

I can't take much more. I know that.

I just can't.

AS SOON AS the car is on the driveway, I get out and follow my father into the house.

"Marie," he shouts. "Are you here?"

My mum comes running from the kitchen, alarmed at my dad's tone. "What's the matter, Ross? Sarah, what are you doing here?"

That's it. I burst into tears. My mum walks over and puts her arm around me.

"I'll let her tell you herself." My dad says, walking over to the freezer and rummaging around. "Where are the peas?" He says in an exasperated manner.

"Well I know you're not cooking the bloody dinner, so just what is going on?" My mum drops her arm from around me, walking over to my father then pushes him out of the way and pulls up his arm.

"You've hit someone?" Her mouth gapes open. "Who?"

"Emmett." He struggles to say through clenched teeth. Mum sighs and grabs a packet from the freezer. She walks over to the counter and grabs the tea-towel, wraps the peas in it and hands it to him.

"Go into the living room and spend time with your granddaughter." She orders.

She waits a minute or two until she knows the coast is clear and then she pulls out a chair at the dining table.

"Sit down. I'll make us both a drink and then you'd better tell me why your father has punched his friend, although I can hazard a guess after last night."

I take the chair and wait while my mum makes two cups of tea. It's so very British to make tea in a crisis.

"Okay, tell me everything." She says sitting next to me. So I do.

"Oh, Sarah." Mum strokes my arm. "What a mess."

"I know. Like Dad said to me, I just escaped the accusation of smacking a kid and then I go and mess up my new employment." I sniffle.

"Sarah. Emmett is a grown man. It took two of you to decide to take things further."

"You said you could guess after last night. What did you mean?"

She takes a sip of tea. "We saw Scott who used

to live next door. I didn't recognise him, but he recognised us."

"Oh yeah, I forgot to tell you he worked there."

"He came over and chatted for a little while. He said you'd been out for a catch up and I said something when he left about there maybe being a potential romance there. Emmett had seemed tense throughout, showed no interest in Celia almost to a point of rudeness, and looked like he was going to punch Scott straight in the nose. I'm not stupid. I could see something was going on, but I didn't know if it was just Emmett developing feelings for you."

"So come on then. Tell me how stupid I've been. I'm ready for it." I sighed.

"Sarah, you have grown up into the most wonderful woman. I know I'm biased because you're my daughter, but you're beautiful and any man would be lucky to have you. It doesn't surprise me at all that Emmett has fallen for you."

I narrowed my gaze. "I don't think using me for fun is quite falling for me."

"I don't know why he said that, but I don't believe it, Sarah. Emmett has dated no one since he lost Louisa to our knowledge. He's let another woman come into his life to care for his two babies, and then he sleeps with her for fun? I'm not buying it. Not one bit."

"You think he was lying?" I hold my breath waiting for her response.

Mum shrugs her shoulders. "I can only guess based on what I know of him and what you're telling me, but it's not adding up to me."

I exhale in a sigh. "Well, it doesn't matter anyway. I'm going to look for yet another new job, somewhere where I can't bump into Emmett. I'm going to make sure I don't find the dad the slightest bit attractive. Then hopefully my dad can manage to get his friendship back on track."

My mum huffs loudly. "Sarah, if you have feelings for Emmett you need to go and tell him. Then if he's definitely not interested, I support you all the way in starting afresh, although please don't move so far away this time, because I like to see you; you're actually the sensible one."

I raise a brow.

"Your dad's just going to have to fucking grow a pair."

My mouth drops open at that and then I start giggling.

"Well, it's true. I know it's a lot for a dad to understand, that his daughter has sex, and I know it's his mate, but if you two have a future then I'm sorry but your dad is going to have to adjust to the new situation. I mean, not being funny, but if a widower has a new chance at love, then your dad having a mardy about his friendship changing seems a little juvenile."

"I really wasn't expecting you to say all this, Mum, to be honest. I thought you'd lecture me like he did."

"You can't help who you fall in love with, darling. Look at me, I still love your dad. Speaking of who, I'd better go calm him down, look after his injuries and somehow get him to realise that his daughter is all grown up."

She leaves me, patting me on the shoulder tenderly as she goes, and I think over her words

'You can't help who you fall in love with'.

Is that what I'm doing? Is it true that Emmett might not have meant what he said? For the first time since my dad hit him, I feel a little tingle of hope. I decide to sleep on things and then see what the morning brings. But I know one thing, I'm not sleeping on the sofa tonight.

Walking into the living room, I find my mum and dad on their way out. "We're off out for a walk." She announces.

. . .

I SIT on the chair in the room. The minute they're gone my brother starts.

"Come on then. What have you done now?"

I turn to him, and Liv who's sat watching the TV with a sleeping Marley at her side. "Can I have a word with you both?" I lean over for the remote and turn it to mute.

Liv begins to look annoyed. "I was watching that."

"Yeah, well this is more important than Coronation Street."

They both turn to me.

"I've had some crap happen to me lately." I begin. "One thing not my fault, the other entirely my fault. But I came home and had to sleep on the sofa because you were here."

My brother opens his mouth, but I raise a hand. "Let me finish."

"Now I don't know how long I'm staying this time. Hopefully just tonight, but if not, you're going to have to move Marley into the larger room with you and put up with it. I'll take your smaller room and put up with that."

"But..."

"But what? This isn't your house. It's mum and dad's, and to be honest we're all grown up. Neither of us should be here. Do you know what dad said to me earlier? He leaves Mum behind to escape to his friend's house to get some peace. He should have peace in his own home. We shouldn't be staying here, Luke."

"They like seeing Marley."

"They do. But you should be visiting with her, not living here. You're having another baby. What are you doing to look for another home, another job? And Liv, I know you don't feel great at the moment, but I'm sure you're capable of cooking a meal or doing some laundry if you're staying for a while. Everyone's treating you like some kind of King and Queen, and do you know why? Because they're scared of upsetting you because you'll kick off. Mum and Dad worry that then you'll punish them by not letting them see Marley. They're walking on eggshells around you. Well, I'm telling you now, you're going to be the parents of two children. Grow the f up."

"It's none of your business, Sarah." Luke lashes out. "You're just sulking because you've had to sleep on the sofa."

Liv turns around to him and places a hand on his arm.

"No, Luke. What Sarah's just said makes a lot of sense."

No one is more surprised than me by Liv's statement. Luke's eyes are wide.

"If you're still here tomorrow we'll all move into your larger room. Maybe if things become a little more uncomfortable for Luke he might go look for a job, instead of feeling like he's having a holiday."

"Oh it's 'get at Luke' time is it?"

"No, not at all. I haven't been pulling my weight either, but in all fairness, Sarah, when you have morning sickness that lasts all day you might understand things a bit better. I'm exhausted. But Luke could wash up some dishes instead of going to the pub."

"I'm sorry, Liv. You're right. And I'm sorry for my outburst. It's been a rough day and I'm taking it out on you."

I lay back in the chair and sigh.

"You need to talk?" Liv asks.

My brother gets up. "Girly talk. I'm out of here."

He gets up and leaves the room.

"I really am sorry, Liv."

"Why? Because you gave us a few harsh truths? I'm not, and Luke needed to hear it. So anyway, what have you done because your dad's excuse of helping Emmett build something for the twins and accidentally hitting his hand with a hammer isn't adding up."

"I slept with Emmett." I confess.

The door swings open and my brother strolls in looking smug. "Who said eavesdropping's a bad thing? Sarah the goody-goody daughter boffed dad's best mate. Oh God, you've done it this time. I'll look like an angel." He chuckles and then he notices Liv's expression.

"Think I'll pop out to see if there are any jobs going, shall I?" He smiles sweetly and reverses back out of the room, though he mimes doubling over with laughter in the doorway where Liv can't see him.

"Now tell me everything." Liv says, and for the first time in a long time, I feel a different vibe forming between me and my brother's girlfriend.

22

EMMETT

Before I do anything else, I've got a visit to make. I wrap both myself and the twins up before placing them both in their buggy and we all brave the bitterly cold morning. The sky is perfectly clear and the grass twinkles in the low sunlight as we make our way down the road. It's the kind of winter morning that Louisa used to love. She used to insist that we wrap up and go for a walk every weekend we were graced with weather like this. I used to love the pink cheeks she used to get as the cold hit her milky skin.

My heart aches with memories of her but unlike many, many times before I'm not filled with grief and sorrow but happiness. At some point I seem to have turned the corner and I am now about to remember our time together with fondness, not just sadness. It's a nice feeling after so long.

It's only a ten-minute walk to the cemetery she loved via the florist across the road. I know that's a weird thing to say but she loved this little church. It was where we said our vows and where she'd always planned to have our babies christened. I followed through with her plans and at six months old, both our babies were christened here with their mother looking over us all.

Even now as I walk past the centuries old headstones, a lump climbs up my throat for everything the four of us lost the day she didn't wake up. I don't think it's something I'll ever properly deal with, but it's a good feeling knowing that I'm able to move on and find another piece of happiness. It's what she'd want.

I bring the buggy to a stop beside her resting place and put the brake on.

"Say hello to your mummy, kiddos." I know they've no idea what I'm talking about. There's no way they understand, but it makes me feel a little better about the whole thing. I never want to hide the truth from them. Even if I get what I want with Sarah, no one will ever replace their mother, something that I already know Sarah appreciates and agrees with from just being their nanny.

As I stand in front of her headstone, I read the engraved words on the front for the millionth time.

Louisa Wilson, beloved wife and mother. Always in our hearts.

I'm immediately taken back to the moment the doctors told me that she didn't make it. I thought it was a joke, a sick one; but a joke nonetheless. I didn't think that kind of thing happened these days. Women didn't die in childbirth. Our healthcare system was too good, so I thought. Unfortunately, Louisa was just not destined to be the mother she'd always craved.

Blowing out a long breath, I prepare to say the words I've come here to say.

"I've met someone, Lou. She's... she's incredible and I think I'm in love with her. But... I just needed you to know before I go and fight for her. I know you'll understand. You'd have wanted me to move on and to find happiness, and you'd want your babies to have a mother figure in their lives. But I just need you to know that you'll always be a part of me. It's just... it's time, Lou."

I hate to stop, the ball of emotion clogging my throat is too large to allow me to get any more words out. The twins babble between each other. It's almost as if they're talking to her too, which only makes my eyes burn that much more but I needed this. I needed to tell her, I needed to let her go and assure her that her spirit will always live on through me and the twins.

Once I'm feeling a little more stable, we say goodbye and take the long way home to make the most of the winter sun.

The twins quickly fall asleep. Making the most of the quiet, I pull my phone from my pocket and call the first estate agent I find on Google.

I explain to the woman on the other end of the phone that I'm looking to sell my house and buy another. She asks me all the relevant questions about my home and I can hear her tapping away on her computer as I talk. We arrange a date for someone to come around to evaluate my house and to take photographs for the listing.

"Okay that's great, Mr Wilson. Before I let you go, what is it you're looking for in your next property? I can see what we've got that might fit your requirements and send you some options to look though."

Pushing the key into the lock, I fumble with the

double buggy and my phone to get inside the house as I consider what I want.

"I need a family home. I've got one-year-old twins. Ideally four bedrooms, a large garden, kitchen diner, a playroom would be incredible, and in commuter distance into the city."

"Okay, great. We've actually got a couple of properties that are yet to be listed that might be of interest to you. Give me thirty minutes and I'll email you some information over. How does that sound?"

"Sounds, perfect. Thank you so—" My words falter when I push the living room door open and find Sarah sitting on my sofa with tears filling her eyes.

I don't say anymore, instead I hang up and drop my phone into my pocket.

"You're selling the house?"

"Yeah, I thought—"

"It was all a bit of fun. I know what you thought," she snaps, not allowing me to tell her my real reasons. As her first tear drops she goes to storm past me. Unlucky for her, I'm faster. My hand wraps around her waist and I pull her in front of me.

Refusing to look up, I lift my hand to her cheek

and gently tilt her head up so she's no choice but to look at me.

"I lied, Sarah. I thought it was in your best interests, but the second you walked out, I knew I'd fucked up." Her lip trembles, another tear dropping but her lips stay sealed. "Yes, I'm putting the house on the market, but not because I'm leaving, but because I think it's time to get a real fresh start, for me and the twins, and for us?"

"Us," she whispers, her eyes wide like she can't believe I just said the word.

"If you'll have me."

"Emmett, I don't know what to say."

"Say yes. Say you'll come house shopping with me and together we can find our new family home. Our fresh start."

"Oh my god," she sobs.

"Is that a yes?"

She doesn't answer with words. Instead, she lifts up on her tiptoes and presses her lips against mine. My hands land on her waist, my fingers pushing the fabric of her top up slightly so I can feel the warmth of her skin as I press her up against the wall. The position isn't all that different from the last time I touched her, but I already know it's going to end differently.

"Fuck," I moan as my lips trail down her neck, her scent filling my nose and her curves under my hands. I thought I'd fucked this up, that I wasn't going to get this chance again.

"Emmett."

Lifting up, I place my forehead against hers. Our breaths mingle as our chests heave but our eyes stay locked on each other's. "I've fallen in love with you."

Her breath catches, her teeth sinking into her bottom lip and she waits as if she thinks I'm going to tell her I'm joking any second.

"Sarah?"

"Shhh, no more words." Her fingers land on my lips to stop me saying anything else. "Just show me."

Pulling her hand down, I slam my lips against hers, making quick work of pushing her skirt up and over her hips and lifting her against the wall. Her legs wrap around my waist, my cock pressing against her core making her moan.

I rock against her, making her back arch and her tits thrust into my face. I bite her covered peak into my mouth as she moans loudly.

"I fucking need you."

"So take me."

Her feet push at the waistband of my jogging bottoms, hoping that she can push them down to get what she needs. I help her out and allow the fabric to drop to my ankles, freeing my needy cock.

"I'll make love to you later," I promise as I pull the lace of her knickers aside and run my swollen head through her wetness.

"Fuck me, Emmett. Fuck me."

"Anything you want."

I thrust up inside her in one swift move and she cries out my name. Her heels dig into my arse and her fingers sink into my hair to hold on as I up my tempo.

She should be quiet, the twins are only sleeping a few feet away, but fuck if I have it in me to care. I need her something vicious. I'll worry about reality once I've felt her pussy clenching around me and she's full of my seed.

"I'm never letting you fucking go again."

"Fuck. Fuck. Fuck," she chants, telling me that she's close. I drop her down the wall a little and thrust that little bit deeper to ensure she finds her release. Not two seconds later, she's crying out as she falls over the edge, causing me to fall with her.

Her head lands on my shoulder as she tries to catch her breath.

ANGEL DEVLIN & TRACY LORRAINE

I've no idea how long we stay frozen in that position, but I couldn't care. It's exactly where I should be.

When she pulls her head from my neck and looks into my eyes, I swear I fall in love with her all over again. Her eyes are soft and glassy from her orgasm but it's more than that, there's something else there.

"Emmett." My breath catches like I know something big is about to happen, something life changing. "I love you too."

EPILOGUE
SARAH

I didn't need my brother to move his daughter to make space for me at home after all. After calling my mum, she agreed I should stay where I was and she'd talk to my father. Emmett had suggested we call around to theirs to talk about things, but my mum felt it was too soon.

I'd like to say everything was a breeze, but it would be a lie.

The house eventually sold, but the house I'd had my heart set on, a beautiful detached house within thirty minutes' drive of my parents' house had fallen through. We'd ended up in a small rental. Living in a home furnished by someone else, and having to put things in storage, meant

Emmett had the task of going through all his house and having to part with many things that had an emotional attachment to Louisa.

I received a letter of apology via my parents' address from the family who'd sacked me, along with a cheque for my owed wages. I banked my wages because I'd earned that money and I'd thrown the letter in the bin. I'd always be bitter about what happened, even though their actions had led me to Emmett.

The twins began toddling around and getting into everything, and because our romance had happened so fast, at times I felt detached. I'd look around us living in a space where we clearly didn't belong and I was having to get used to being somewhere between a lover and a nanny. At what point did we discuss him stopping paying me? How would this house be our family home when I couldn't contribute? My career was in childcare.

After looking at other houses that weren't quite right, we finally settled on one that although wasn't my dream house, we could make a home in. Emmett took care of all the legal side of things while I avoided that awkward situation that I knew was going to come up soon. We were in love. Absolutely head over heels in love. And we were going to move in together; but if things continued to get serious, I couldn't be paid to nanny children I wanted to be the mother to. And I did. I loved these children with every part of my being.

Emmett decided he wanted to show my parents and his mother our new house. I was annoyed because I'd wanted to go and measure up curtains and things but there'd been some kind of hold up and so Emmett had told me that we wouldn't be able to sort anything out until after it had all gone through. We still had two months on the rental, so we had some time, but still. I felt I belonged nowhere and it was starting to get to me.

Emmett, the twins, and I piled into his 4x4 and he began driving us. The house was again about thirty minutes away from my parents' but as we approached the junction we should take, Emmett suddenly went a different way.

"Where are you going? That's not the way to the house."

He turned to me and smirked.

"What are you up to, Mr Wilson?"

My heart began to beat faster because I knew what I hoped for and if it wasn't, I didn't think I could take it.

But I was right, as Emmett turned the corner and our original dream house came into view.

"What?" I sat up straighter. "I don't understand. Is this really ours?"

Emmett jumped out of the car, came around to my side and opened the door. "The sale they had fell through. The estate agent phoned and I immediately made them an offer, a good one, with the proviso that it was a done deal. They accepted."

"And you didn't tell me? You led me to believe it was the other one." I shoved him in the arm. "You utter twat."

"Now, now, children are listening." He smiled. "Let's get them and go see our new home."

But instead of getting out a key, he just pushed open the door and said 'after you'. I walked in to find the hallway full of red roses. They were everywhere, in vases, and rose petals were strewn across the floor. I followed the trail into the living room.

"Auntie Saywah." Marley shouted, running up to me. "There's a big secret and I can't tell it you at all."

"That's because you haven't been told it

either." Liv laughed, coming over and taking her hand.

"Oh it is a big secret." I said. "Auntie Sarah was not expecting to get this big house." I said hello to everyone there. They all congratulated me on the new home and laughed with me about how I'd been fooled.

My dad embraced me. Things had taken time, longer with him than anyone else. It wasn't surprising. After a lot of discussion, my father and Emmett had decided that as the business was doing so well, they'd split it into two parts, small business and larger ones. Emmett took on the small business part and they separated the two companies though still operated under one umbrella name. It stopped my dad having to be Emmett's employer as well as the father of his girlfriend. Even more surprisingly, my brother Luke had started work there after confessing that he hadn't been sneaking out to the pub but had been doing a computer course. He'd not wanted to tell anyone in case he didn't pass, because he'd have felt embarrassed. He had however had a pint or two on the way home. Him and Liv had a new rental now and her belly was blooming.

ANGEL DEVLIN & TRACY LORRAINE

"Your new house is beautiful." My father told me.

"Thanks, Dad." I smiled. "I just know I'm going to be really happy here."

"I'm sure you will be." He hugged me. "I know Emmett is a good man. It just took me a while to get used to him being your good man. He's still aware that if he ever hurts you, I'll hit him again."

I rolled my eyes and laughed.

"Oh, it looks like your boyfriend wants to make a toast." Dad nodded his head towards Emmett who stood in front of the living room mantelshelf.

Emmett rubbed the back of his neck, then stood looking around at everyone. Then he swallowed. "Thank you all for being here today and for keeping my big secret. I'm sure Sarah will back me up here when I say living with two walking toddlers in a small rental has not been plain sailing. However hopefully from today we can get on with the rest of our lives in our beautiful new home."

He beckoned towards me. "If you could come over here, Sarah."

Oh God, I hope I didn't have to talk.

But as I approached, I realised I'd got it all wrong. The house wasn't the big secret after all.

Because Emmett dropped to one knee. My hand flew to my mouth as I gasped. I was shaking as he took my hand in his.

"Sarah, they say home is where the heart is. But it's not where mine is. My heart is with you. It belongs to you and our children."

Our children.

"With the blessing of your father," Emmett laughs. "I'm asking, will you marry me?"

"Yes." I cried.

Everyone around us applauded. Then my brother coughed.

"While we're here." He dropped to his own knee in front of Liv. "Oh good God," my mother hissed.

"Liv, you are carrying our second child. I promise to work hard and love you all forever. Will you marry me?"

Liv pulled Luke up from the floor. "No, I bloody will not, you great idiot. This is your sister's proposal. Since when has a woman wanted her man to impulsively propose on the floor of someone else's home? You need to work on a better, more romantic proposal than that." She walked off and my mum and dad shook their heads in an 'only Luke' way as Luke went running off after her.

Marley ran after her dad. "I'll marry you, Daddy."

Everyone left after a couple of hours and then it was just me, Emmett, and the twins. "I rented the furniture for this room. It goes back in the morning." He told me. "So we need to go shopping as soon as possible and get moved in as soon as possible."

"I love you, Emmett Wilson." I threw my arms around him and got on my tiptoes to kiss him.

"I love you too."

"What's going to happen in the future though? How will I pay my way?"

"What are you talking about? You look after the kids."

"Yes, but that was my job. To be their nanny. Now I'm going to be in a mum role when we get married."

Emmett laughed. "Sarah, what are you talking about? You've been in a mum role with these babies since you arrived. And yes I paid you because I employed you as their nanny, and I know it got complicated when we started dating, but as far as I'm concerned, we have the business and the home and we'll run them between us. I need someone to do the books so I can concentrate on the work and we have the children. Our money is our money."

"I just feel like I'm sponging off you."

"And I feel like I'm taking advantage because you've always done far more than your billable hours, but do you know what?"

"What?"

"I like taking advantage of you, and soon I'm going to take advantage of you in every room of this house."

"Okay, I think I can live with us taking advantage of each other." I said, and then Emmett's mouth closed down on mine.

Two years later

We married in the summer, the year after our engagement. It was a beautiful ceremony and I had the cutest bridesmaids and pageboy in the universe. Marley held a hand of each twin as she walked down the aisle behind me, while Bree toddled behind them.

Everything had changed after we'd moved into our new home. I immediately felt settled in the place that was ours and the fact we kept talking about issues so honestly as they came up meant our relationship got stronger.

Our biggest hurdle came just after the

wedding, when I found out I was pregnant. Emmett freaked out completely. Scared I was going to die, to leave him and the twins. He'd had to have counselling around things and it had been a difficult time, but eventually he'd realised that tragedy can strike at any time; it didn't need to wait for childbirth.

Yesterday, my waters had broken and this morning I had given birth to Lana. Emmett was besotted. I turned to him now as he cradled our daughter. I'd decided to stick with another L name and I hoped Louisa was looking down at us somewhere happy as she saw the twins peeking at their baby sister.

We'd agreed Emmett would have a vasectomy now. Our family was complete and I didn't want Emmett to go through the trauma of another pregnancy with me.

Our relationship had started out forbidden, the nanny and her employer, but as I stared at my husband and my babies and thought about the challenges we'd faced to get here, I knew I wouldn't change a single thing.

Because love isn't all rosy, even if your husband brings you a bunch of red ones at the beginning of every week.

THE END

Are you ready for the EPIC finale to the Hot Daddy Series?

It's time for Scott and Suki!

GRAB HOT DADDY PACKAGE NOW!

ABOUT ANGEL DEVLIN

Angel Devlin writes stories as hot as her coffee. She lives in Sheffield with her partner, son, and a gorgeous whippet called Bella.

Newsletter:
Sign up here for Angel's latest news and exclusive content.
https://geni.us/angeldevlinnewsletter

ABOUT TRACY LORRAINE

Tracy Lorraine is new adult and contemporary romance author. Tracy is in her thirties and lives in a cute Cotswold village in England with her husband and daughter. Having always been a bookaholic with her head stuck in her Kindle, Tracy decided to try her hand at a story idea she dreamt up and hasn't looked back since.

Be the first to find out about new releases and offers. Sign up to my newsletter here.

If you want to know what I'm up to and see teasers and snippets of what I'm working on, then you need to be in my Facebook group. Join Tracy's Angels here.

Keep up to date with Tracy's books at
www.tracylorraine.com